STORIES

for Girls

Illustrated by
Jeremy Bays, Natalie Bould, Lynn Breeze, Anna Cattermole,
Maureen Galvani, Mary Hall, Virginia Margerison, Paula Martyr,
Julia Oliver, Martin Orme, Sara Silcock, Gillian Toft, Charlie Ann Turner,
Kerry Vaughan, Jenny Williams and Kirsty Wilson

This is a Parragon Book
This edition published in 2004

Parragon
Queen Street House
4 Queen Street
Bath BA1 1HE, UK

Printed and bound in Dubai
ISBN 1-40544-307-3

STORIES

for Girls

Written by Derek Hall, Alison Morris and Louisa Somerville

Contents

Mrs Mouse's Holiday

Mrs Mouse was very excited. All year she had been *so* busy. First there had been nuts and berries to gather in readiness for winter. Then she had needed to give her little house a big spring clean to make it nice and fresh. Now, as the warm sun shone down on the trees and flowers of her woodland home, she had promised herself a well-deserved holiday. But getting ready for holidays seemed to make one busier than ever! There was so much to do!

First she took out her little case, opened it and placed it carefully on her neatly made bed. Then she rushed to her cupboard and selected some fine holiday dresses. Back to her case she scuttled and laid them in. Now she chose several pairs of shoes – a nice pair of sandals for walking along the front in,

a pair of smart shoes for shopping in,
an even smarter pair for going to dinner
in, and another pair just in case!

"I'll need a couple of sun hats,"
she thought to herself, and so into
the case they went as well. These were followed by a coat, some
gloves and a scarf (just in case the breeze got up and it became
cold). Then, in case it became very sunny, in went some
sunglasses, some sun cream and a sunshade. But, oh dear, there
were so many things in the case that it refused to shut. She tried
sitting on it, and bouncing on it, but still it stubbornly would
not close.

So out from the case came all the things that she had just put
in, and Mrs Mouse scurried to the cupboard again and chose an
even bigger case. This time they all fitted perfectly, and she shut
the case with a big sigh of relief.

Now she was ready to go to the seaside for her holiday. She
sat on the train, with her case on the rack above her head,
munching her hazel nut sandwiches and looking eagerly out of
the window hoping to see the sea. Finally, as the train chuffed
around a bend, there it was! A great, deep blue sea shimmering
in the sun, with white gulls soaring over the cliffs and headlands.

"I'm really looking forward to a nice, quiet rest," she said
to herself.

Her guest house was very comfortable, and so close to the sea that she could smell the clean, salty air whenever she opened her window. "This is the life," she thought. "Nice and peaceful."

After she had put her clothes away, she put on her little swimming costume and her sun hat and packed her beach bag. Now she was ready for some peaceful sunbathing!

At the beach, she found herself a quiet spot, closed her eyes and was soon fast asleep. But not for long! A family of voles had arrived on the beach, and they weren't trying to have a quiet time at all. The youngsters in the family yelled at the top of their voices, splashed water everywhere, and sent their beach ball tumbling all over Mrs Mouse's neatly laid out beach towel.

Just as Mrs Mouse thought that it couldn't get any noisier, along came a crowd of ferrets. Now if you've ever sat on a beach next to a crowd of ferrets, you'll know what it's like. Their noisy shouting and singing made Mrs Mouse's head buzz.

Mrs Mouse couldn't stand it a moment longer. She was just wondering where she might find some peace and quiet when she spotted a rock just a little way out to sea.

"If I swim out to that rock," she thought, "I will surely have some peace and quiet there." So she gathered up her belongings and swam over to the rock. It was a bit lumpy, but at least it was quiet. Soon she was fast asleep again.

Just then the rock started to move slowly out to sea! It wasn't really a rock at all, you see, but a turtle which had been dozing near the surface. Off into the sunset it went, with Mrs Mouse dozing on its back, quite unaware of what was happening.

9

Eventually, the turtle came to a deserted island. At that moment, Mrs Mouse woke up. She looked at the empty beach, and without even knowing she had been sleeping on a turtle, she jumped off and swam to the shore, thinking it was the beach that she had just left.

Just then, the turtle swam off, and Mrs Mouse suddenly realised what had happened. For a moment she was horrified. But then she looked at the quiet, palm–fringed beach with no-one about but herself, and thought of the noisy beach she had just left.

"Well, perhaps this isn't such a bad place to spend a quiet holiday after all," she thought.

10

And that's just what she did. Day after day she lazed on her own private beach with no–one to disturb her. There were plenty of coconuts and fruits to eat, and she wanted for nothing. She even made herself a cozy bed from palm leaves.

Eventually, though, she started to miss her own little house in the woods and decided it was time to get back home. First she took half a coconut and nibbled out the tasty inside. "That will make a fine boat to sit in," she said.

Next she found a palm leaf and stuck it in the bottom of the shell. She took her little boat to the water's edge and, as the wind caught her palm leaf sail, off she floated back to the boarding house to get her belongings.

As she sailed back she thought, "This is the quietest holiday I've ever had. I may come back here next year!"

Lucy and the Green Door

Lucy Jenkins lived in an ordinary house, in an ordinary street, in an ordinary town. At the back of Lucy's house was an ordinary garden with ordinary flowers and an ordinary path. But down the path at the bottom of the garden was a tree that was not ordinary at all! It was a huge old oak tree, and at the bottom of the tree was a very small green door, only just big enough for Lucy to squeeze through. This was Lucy's secret, because only she knew about the door. But what lay behind the door was Lucy's best secret of all!

Each afternoon Lucy would go down the garden path and knock lightly on the door. On the third knock the door would swing open wide, and the chief elf would be there to welcome her inside.

"Come inside, little Lucy," the elf would always say, "and have some tea."

Inside, Lucy would meet some very special friends indeed! First there were Penelope and Geraldine, two of the gentlest and sweetest fairies it was possible to imagine. Then there were Basil and Granville, who were rather mischievous imps (but who made Lucy laugh with their tricks and jokes), and there were the storytellers, who would sit for hours with Lucy and tell her the greatest tales from all the corners of the world. And of course there was the chief elf, who would make the most delicious milk shakes and scones with heaps of cream for Lucy to eat.

The world behind the green door was a wonderful place, and Lucy would always go home afterwards feeling very cheerful and jolly. On one particular visit to the world behind the green door Lucy had just finished a scrumptious tea of cocoa and toasted marshmallows with the chief elf, when she went off to play games with Basil and Granville. They were playing blind man's buff, and Lucy roared with laughter as Basil sneaked up on the blindfolded Granville and tickled him in the ribs, making him squeal and beg for the teasing to stop.

13

Now just recently, Lucy had been feeling down in the dumps because very soon she would be going to school and would only be able to visit her friends at weekends. But they assured her that they would never forget her, and that as long as she was always a true friend to them she could visit as often or as little as she liked. This cheered Lucy up considerably, and then they took her to visit the storytellers so that her happiness was complete. Of all the delights behind the green door, the storytellers were Lucy's favourite. They told her stories of how the whales had learned to sing, and of where the stars went when the sun had risen in the sky and they had slipped from view.

Because of the assurances of the fairies, Lucy was not too worried when the day finally came for her to join all the other boys and girls of her age at school. Every day, Lucy would go to school and then afterwards would visit her friends behind the green door. As winter came round and the days grew dark she only visited at weekends, and looked forward to the holidays when she could visit them every day once more.

Meanwhile, at school, Lucy had made friends with a girl called Jessica, and although she told Jessica all about her family and her home, she didn't at first tell her about her extraordinary tree with the little green door and the magic world that lay beyond. Lucy did tell Jessica all the stories that she was told by the storytellers, however, and Jessica grew more and more curious about where she had heard all the wonderful tales. Every day, Jessica would ask more and more questions, and Lucy found it more and more difficult to avoid telling her about her secret. Eventually, Lucy gave in and told Jessica all about her adventures behind the green door.

Jessica scoffed and laughed when Lucy told her about the chief elf, and Basil, Granville, Penelope and Geraldine. She howled with laughter at the thought of the wonderful teas and the stories that followed. Jessica thought that Lucy was making the whole thing up! When Lucy protested, and said it was true, Jessica told her that it simply wasn't possible – that there were no such things as elves and fairies and imps and strange and wonderful worlds behind doors in trees. Lucy was distraught, and decided to take Jessica to the green door.

On the way home Lucy started to worry. What if she really had imagined it all? But if her wonderful friends didn't exist, how could she possibly know them? Jessica walked beside Lucy, still teasing her and laughing about Lucy's 'invisible' friends!

When Lucy and Jessica reached the bottom of the garden, Lucy was about to tap lightly on the green door at the bottom of the oak tree when she suddenly noticed the door had disappeared. She rubbed her eyes and looked again, but it simply wasn't there!

Jessica smirked and laughed at Lucy, calling her silly and babyish to believe in magic and fairy tales, and then ran off back down the road to school. Lucy could not face going back to school that afternoon, and when her mother saw her enter the house she thought she must be ill – she looked so upset! Lucy went to bed early and cried herself to sleep.

And when Lucy slept she started to dream. The chief elf, Basil and Granville, Penelope and Geraldine and the storytellers were all there in the dream. Then Penelope and Geraldine stepped forward and hugged Lucy, and the hug was so real that

Lucy began to hope it wasn't a dream! Then they all hugged her and asked why she hadn't been to see them for so long, and why they had not been able to reach out to her except now in the deepest of sleeps. Lucy explained what had happened on her last visit, and told them all about Jessica, and then Geraldine spoke. "Little Lucy," she said, "you are special. You believe in magic and you believe in the little people. And because you believe, you are able to see us and live among us. But those who don't believe will always be shut out from our world. You must keep your belief, little Lucy."

With a huge surge of happiness Lucy woke up, dressed quickly and ran out of her ordinary house, down the ordinary path in the ordinary garden up to the extraordinary tree, and was delighted to see the green door once more! She knocked very lightly and, after the third tap, the door swung open to reveal the chief elf. "Come inside, little Lucy," the elf said happily, "and have some tea."

The Red Daffodil

It was spring time and all the daffodils were pushing their heads up towards the warmth of the sun. Slowly, their golden petals unfolded to let their yellow trumpets dance in the breeze. One particular field of daffodils was a blaze of gold like all the others – but right in the middle was a single splash of red. For there in the middle was a red daffodil.

From the moment she opened her petals, the red daffodil knew she was different from the other flowers. They sneered at her and whispered to each other. "What a strange, poor creature!" said one.

"She must envy our beautiful golden colour," said another.

18

And indeed it was true. The red daffodil wished very much that she was like the others. Instead of being proud of her red petals, she was ashamed and hung her head low. "What's wrong with me?" she thought. "Why aren't there any other red daffodils in the field?"

Passers-by stopped to admire the field of beautiful daffodils. "What a wonderful sight!" they exclaimed. And the daffodils' heads swelled with pride and danced in the breeze all the more merrily.

Then someone spotted the red daffodil right in the middle of the field. "Look at that extraordinary flower!" the man shouted. Everyone peered into the centre of the field.

"You're right," said someone else, "there's a red daffodil in the middle." Soon a large crowd had gathered, all pointing and laughing at the red daffodil.

She could feel herself blushing even redder at the attention. "How I wish my petals would close up again," she said to herself in anguish. But try as she might, her fine red trumpet stood out for all to see.

Now, in the crowd of people gathered at the edge of the field was a little girl. People were pushing and shoving and she couldn't see anything at all. At last, her father lifted her high upon his shoulders so that she could see into the field. "Oh!" exclaimed the little girl in a very big voice. "So that's the red daffodil. I think it's really beautiful. What a lucky daffodil to be so different."

And do you know, other people heard what the little girl said and they began to whisper to each other, "Well, I must say, I actually thought myself it was rather pretty, you know." Before long, people were praising the daffodil's beauty and saying it must be a very special flower. The red daffodil heard what the crowd was saying. Now she was blushing with pride and held her head as high as all the other daffodils in the field.

The other daffodils were furious. "What a foolish crowd," said one indignantly. "We are the beautiful ones!" They turned their heads away from the red daffodil and ignored her. She began to feel unhappy again.

By now word had spread far and wide about the amazing red daffodil and people came from all over the land to see her. Soon, the king's daughter got to hear about the red daffodil. "I must see this for myself," said the princess. She set off with her servant and eventually they came to the field where the red daffodil grew. When the princess saw her, she clapped her hands with glee.

"The red daffodil is more beautiful than I ever imagined," she cried. Then she had an idea. "Please bring my pet dove," she said to her servant. The man looked rather puzzled, but soon he returned with the bird. "As you know," said the princess to the servant, "I am to be married tomorrow and I would dearly love to have that red daffodil in my wedding bouquet."

The princess sent the dove into the middle of the field and it gently picked up the daffodil in its beak and brought her back to where the princess stood. The princess carried the daffodil back to the palace. She put the daffodil in a vase of water and there she stayed until the next day.

In the morning, the princess's servant took the red daffodil to the church. She could hear the bells and see all the guests assembling for the wedding ceremony. Then she saw the princess arrive in a coach driven by four white horses. How lovely the princess looked in her white gown and her head crowned with deep red roses.

As the servant reached the church door, the princess's lady-in-waiting stepped forward holding a huge bouquet of flowers into which she placed the red daffodil just as the flowers were handed to the princess. For a while, the red daffodil was overcome by the powerful scents of the other flowers in the bouquet, but when at last she looked around her she realised, with astonishment, that all of them were red. There were red daisies, red lilies, red carnations and red foxgloves. "Welcome," said one of the daisies, "you're one of us." And for the first time in her life, the red daffodil felt really at home.

After the wedding, the princess scattered the flowers from her bouquet among the flowers in her garden. Every spring, when she opened her petals, the red daffodil found she was surrounded by lots of other red flowers, and she lived happily in the garden for many, many years.

The Lonely Mermaid

There once lived a mermaid named Miriam who was very lonely. All day long she sat on a rock combing her long, yellow hair and singing to herself. Sometimes she would flick her beautiful turquoise fish tail in the water and watch the ripples spreading far out to sea. Miriam had not always been lonely. In fact, she used to have a pair of playmates called Octopus and Dolphin. Octopus had gone off to another part of the ocean to work for the Sea King. He was always much in demand because he could do eight jobs at once – one with each arm. Dolphin, meanwhile, had gone away to teach singing in a school of dolphins. Miriam once thought she heard his lovely song far away across the ocean and she hoped in vain that he might come back and play.

24

One day Miriam was sitting on her favourite rock as usual. "How lonely I am," she sighed to her reflection as she combed her hair and gazed at herself in the mirror.

To her astonishment, her reflection seemed to answer back. "Don't be lonely," said a voice. "Come and play with me."

Miriam couldn't understand it at all. She peered into the mirror and then she saw, beyond her own reflection, another mermaid! She was so startled that she dropped the mirror and her comb and spun around.

Miriam was puzzled by the sight in front of her. For there, sitting on the next rock was another mermaid – and yet she didn't look like a mermaid in many ways. She had short, dark, curly hair and wore a strange costume that definitely wasn't made of seaweed. When Miriam looked down to where the mermaid's fish tail should have been, she wanted to burst out laughing.

For instead of a beautiful tail, the other mermaid had two strange limbs like an extra long pair of arms stretching down.

The other 'mermaid', who was really a little girl called Georgie, was equally amazed by the sight of Miriam. She had seen pictures of mermaids in books before, but now she couldn't quite believe her eyes. For here, on the rock beside her, was a real live mermaid!

For a moment they were both too astonished to speak. Then they both said at once, "Who are you?"

"I'm Miriam," said Miriam.

"I'm Georgie," said Georgie.

"Let's go for a swim," said Miriam. Soon the two of them were in the water, chasing each other and giggling.

"Let's play tag along the beach," suggested Georgie, and started swimming towards the shore. She had quite forgotten that Miriam would not be able to run around on dry land. Miriam followed though she was rather afraid, as her mother had always told her not to go near the shore in case she got stranded. Georgie ran out of the water and up on to the beach.

"Wait for me!" called Miriam, struggling in the water as her tail thrashed about. Then, to her astonishment, something strange happened. She found she could leave the water with ease and, looking down, saw that her tail had disappeared and that in its place were two of those strange long arm things like Georgie's

"What's happened?" she wailed.

Georgie looked round. "You've grown legs!" she shouted in amazement. "Now you can play tag!"

Miriam found that she rather liked having legs. She tried jumping in the air, and Georgie taught her to hop and skip. "You can come and stay at my house, but first I must find you some clothes," said Georgie, looking at Miriam who was wearing nothing but her long, yellow hair. "Wait for me here!"

Georgie ran off and soon she was back with a tee shirt and shorts. Miriam put them on. They ran back to Georgie's house together. "This is my friend Miriam," said Georgie to her mother. "Can she stay for tea?"

"Why, of course," said Georgie's mother.

"What's that strange thing?" whispered Miriam.

"It's a chair," said Georgie. She showed Miriam how to sit on the chair. All through teatime Miriam watched Georgie to see how she should eat from a plate and drink from a cup and saucer. She'd never tasted food like this before. How she wished she could have chocolate cake at home under the sea!

After tea Miriam said, "Now I'll show *you* how to do something." Taking Georgie by the hand she led her down to the beach again. There they picked up shells, and then Miriam showed Georgie how to make a lovely necklace from shells threaded with seaweed. While they made their necklaces, Miriam taught Georgie how to sing songs of the sea.

Soon it was bedtime. "You can sleep in the spare bed in my room," said Georgie. Miriam slipped in between the sheets. How strange it felt! She was used to feeling water all around her and here she was lying in a bed. She tossed and turned, feeling hotter and hotter, and couldn't sleep at all. In the middle of the night she got up and threw open the window to get some fresh air.

She could smell the salty sea air and she began to feel rather homesick. Then she heard a familiar sound from far away. It was Dolphin calling to her! The noise was getting closer and closer until at last Miriam knew what she must do. She slipped out of the house and ran down to the beach in the moonlight. As soon as her toes touched the water, her legs turned back into a fish tail and she swam out to sea to join Dolphin.

The next morning, when Georgie woke up, she was very upset to find that her friend had gone. When she told her mother who Miriam really was, her mother said, "The sea is a mermaid's true home and that's where she belongs. But I'm sure you two will always be friends."

And indeed, from time to time, Georgie was sure that she could see Miriam waving to her from the sea.

Rapunzel

There once lived a man and his wife who had long wished for a child. At last their wish was granted and the wife found that she was expecting a baby. At the back of their house was a garden that was filled with the most beautiful flowers and herbs. However, the man and his wife did not dare enter the garden, for it was owned by a wicked witch, of whom everyone was scared.

One day, when the woman was standing by her window looking down into the garden, she saw a flower bed full of the prettiest Rapunzel plants she had ever seen. They looked so fresh and green that she felt a great craving to eat some of them. Day after day she would sit by her window, staring at the Rapunzel plants for hours on end. Eventually she became quite pale and miserable.

"What's wrong, my dear?" said her husband.

"I must have some of that Rapunzel," she replied, "or I may die."

The poor husband decided that the only thing to do was to steal into the witch's garden at night and take some of the plants. Late one night the man climbed the high wall that surrounded the garden and hastily snatched a bunch of Rapunzel plants and made off with them.

His wife was delighted. She made a salad of them that was so delicious that the next day she said to her husband, "I must have more of that delicious Rapunzel."

So that night the husband stole once more into the witch's garden. Imagine his horror when he dropped on to the grass to find the witch there lying in wait for him. "How dare you come into my garden and steal my Rapunzel plants," she shrieked. "You'll live to regret this."

"Please have mercy on me," begged the man. "I'm not really a thief. I came to help my wife, who is expecting our first child. She told me she would die if she didn't have some of your Rapunzel to eat."

Then the witch changed her tune. "By all means," she said, "take as much as you like. But in exchange you must give me the baby when it is born. Don't worry – I will care for it as if I were its mother. What do you say?" The man was so terrified that he hastily agreed to what the witch had said. When his wife gave birth to a baby girl the witch immediately appeared to take the child. The witch named her Rapunzel, after the plants that had caused all the trouble, and took the child away with her.

Rapunzel grew very beautiful, strong and
healthy, with long golden hair that fell past her
waist. When she was twelve years old the witch
locked her away at the top of a tower in the
middle of a forest. The tower had neither stairs
nor a door, but only one window at the top so
that nobody but the witch could reach her.

Each day when the witch visited her, she
would stand below the girl's window and call
out, "Rapunzel, Rapunzel, let down your hair,
that I may climb without a stair."

Then the girl would wind her long
tresses around the window hook and
lower her hair all the way to the ground.
The witch would climb up it as if it
were a ladder. In this way,
Rapunzel's lonely life went on
for several years.

One day, a young prince was
riding in the forest when he heard a
sweet voice. It was Rapunzel singing
to herself. The prince was so
entranced that he followed the sound
and came upon the tower.

But when he could find no way in he became discouraged and rode home. Rapunzel's lovely voice had stirred his heart so deeply, however, that he returned day after day to hear her singing.

One day, as he stood behind a tree, he saw the witch appear and heard her calling, "Rapunzel, Rapunzel, let down your hair, that I may climb without a stair."

Then he saw a mass of golden hair tumble down and watched the witch climb up it to the window. "Is that the way up?" thought the prince. "Then I will climb the golden ladder, too."

The next day, around dusk, the prince went to the tower and called, "Rapunzel, Rapunzel, let down your hair, that I may climb without a stair."

34

Immediately the tresses fell down and the prince climbed up. At first sight of the prince, Rapunzel was afraid, but the prince addressed her in such a friendly way that she knew she could trust him. "Once I had heard your voice," said the prince, "I couldn't rest until I saw you. Now I cannot rest until you agree to marry me."

Rapunzel by now had fallen truly in love with the young man, so she willingly accepted. "I wish I could come away with you," said Rapunzel. "You must bring some silk with you each time you visit, and I shall weave a ladder of silk and then I will be able to escape."

Each day the witch visited Rapunzel and each night the prince came. The witch suspected nothing until one day Rapunzel forgot herself and said to the witch, "Why are you so much heavier to pull up than the prince?"

35

"Oh, treacherous girl," screamed the witch. "You have deceived me!" She snatched up a pair of scissors and cut off all Rapunzel's lovely hair. Then the witch drove Rapunzel from the tower and left her in a wild and desolate place to fend for herself as best she could.

That night, along came the prince to the tower and said, as usual, "Rapunzel, Rapunzel, let down your hair, that I may climb without a stair."

But the witch was lying in wait. She tied Rapunzel's hair to the window hook and let the golden tresses fall to the ground. Up climbed the prince full of joy, as always. But when he stepped in through the window, it was not his beautiful Rapunzel that met his gaze but the icy glare of the witch. "Aha!" cried the witch with a sneer. "So you thought you could steal my girl, did you? Well she's gone and you'll never set eyes on her again."

Beside himself with grief, the prince threw himself from the tower and would have died had he not landed in the thickest briars. Although he survived, the thorns pierced his eyes and blinded him. For many years he wandered through the wilderness grieving for his lost Rapunzel and living on whatever he could find to eat. Eventually, he wandered into the same part of the wilderness where Rapunzel lived in miserable poverty with the twins she had borne.

Just as he had done so many years ago, the prince heard a sweet voice coming through the trees. He made his way towards the sound of the voice. Suddenly Rapunzel saw him and straight away she recognised him. She ran to him and threw her arms around him weeping. As she wept tears of joy and sorrow, two teardrops fell into his eyes, healing them and restoring his sight.

Then the two were united again and the prince took Rapunzel and their children back to his own kingdom, and they all lived happily ever after.

The Princess and the Snowman

One morning Princess Bella looked out of her bedroom window and saw that the palace was covered in a thick layer of snow. Snow lay on the turrets and along the tops of the walls. There was snow in the well and snow on the guards' hats. The palace garden was so deep with snow it looked as though it was covered in delicious icing. The snow looked fresh, inviting and untouched – apart from a line of paw prints made by Bella's pet cat, Beau.

The princess clapped her hands with glee. "I'm going to make a snowman," she cried, and rushed off to find her warmest coat and gloves. Soon she was busy in the garden rolling a great ball of snow for the snowman's body and another one for his head.

At last the snowman was finished, and she put an old hat on his head and a scarf around his neck.

"Now," thought Princess Bella, "he needs a face." Turning to Beau she said, "Go and find the snowman a nose."

"Meiow!" said Beau and trotted off. Bella found three lumps of coal and stuck them in a row on the snowman's head to make a mouth. Then she stuck a stone on each side of his head for ears. Beau came back with a piece of carrot in her mouth.

"Well done, Beau," said Bella. "That's perfect for a nose." And she stuck the carrot in place.

At that moment there was a call from a palace window. "Bella, Bella! Come inside at once. It's time for your lessons," called the queen. Bella ran indoors and, do you know, she forgot all about giving the snowman a pair of eyes.

"I wonder when the princess will come and give me my eyes," thought the snowman wistfully. "I'd better keep my wits about me." He listened hard with his stone ears and sniffed with his carrot nose, but there was no-one there.

Night came and all the lights in the palace went out. In the middle of the night, a storm blew up. The windows of the palace rattled, the trees creaked and groaned and the wind moaned. The snowman strained his stone ears even harder and now he could hear a fearsome icy jangle and a piercing, shrieking laugh. It was the Ice Queen. As she blew past the snowman, he felt the Ice Queen's cold breath on his snowy cheek and the touch of her icicle fingers on his snowy brow. The snowman shivered with fear. Now he heard the Ice Queen's icy tap, tap, tap on the palace door and her howl as she slipped through the keyhole. There was silence for a while, then suddenly the snowman heard a window being flung open and the Ice Queen's cruel laugh.

"She's leaving," thought the snowman with relief.

But what was this? Now he could hear the sound of a girl sobbing and as the Ice Queen passed he heard

40

Princess Bella's voice calling, "Help me!" Then there was silence again, save for the sound of the wind in the trees.

"She's carried off the princess," thought the snowman. "There's only one thing to do!" He drew his breath and with all his might he shouted through his coal lips, "Heeelp!" He thought to himself, "No-one will hear my shouts above the noise of the wind."

But soon he felt a warm glow on his cheek. "Can I help?" said a soft, kindly voice. "I am the South Wind and I can see you're in trouble."

The snowman could hardly believe his stone ears. "Oh, yes, please help," he cried. "The Ice Queen has carried off Princess Bella and I'm afraid she may die of cold."

"I'll see what I can do," said the South Wind gently, and she started to blow a warm wind. She blew and she blew and soon the Ice Queen's icy arms began to melt. Then Bella was able to slip from her cold grasp.

"It was the snowman who saved you," whispered the South Wind in Bella's ear as she carried her back to the palace.

Bella could hear the drip, drip, sound of snow being melted by the South Wind's warm breath. As she reached the palace gate, the sun was rising and the snow in the garden was turning to slush. "I must see my snowman before he is gone," she thought.

There he was on the lawn. His hat was starting to slide off his head and his mouth was all crooked. She rushed over to him and to her astonishment he spoke.

"Please give me my eyes before I melt completely," he begged.

"Yes, of course I will," Bella replied. Quickly she fixed two pieces of coal in place on his melting face.

"You are so lovely," said the snowman, looking at her with his coal eyes. "I have one last request before I'm gone. Will you marry me?"

"Why, I will!" said Bella without thinking twice – for how could she refuse the request of the one who had saved her from the Ice Queen?

Bella could not bear to think that the snowman was melting away. She glanced down so that he would not see that she was crying.

"Bella," he said. She looked up and there standing before her was a prince. For once in her life she was speechless.

"Long ago, the Ice Queen carried me away – just like she did to you. She cast a spell on me that meant I could only return to earth as falling snow. But by agreeing to marry me you have broken the spell," said the prince.

And so Bella and the prince were married, and lived happily ever after.

The Frog Prince

There was once a king who had but one daughter. Being his only child, she wanted for nothing. She had a nursery full of toys, a pony to ride and a wardrobe bursting with pretty dresses. But, for all this, the princess was lonely. "How I wish I had someone to play with," she sighed.

The princess's favourite toy was a beautiful golden ball. Every day she would play with her ball in the palace garden. When she threw the ball up in the air, it seemed to take off of its own accord and touch the clouds before landing in the princess's hands again.

One windy day the princess was playing in the garden as usual. She threw her golden ball high into the air, but instead of returning to her hands, the wind blew the ball into the fishpond. The princess ran to the pond, but to her dismay the ball had sunk right to the bottom. "Whatever shall I do?" wailed the girl. "Now I have lost my favourite toy." And she sat down beside the pond and cried.

All at once she heard a loud PLOP! and a large green frog landed on the grass beside her. "Eeeuugh! Go away you nasty thing!" screamed the princess.

To her astonishment, the frog spoke to her. "I heard you crying," he said in a gentle voice, "and I wondered what the matter was. Can I help you in any way?"

45

"Why, yes!" exclaimed the princess, once she had got over the shock of being addressed by a frog. "My ball has sunk to the bottom of the pond. Would you fish it out for me?"

"Of course I will," replied the frog. "But in return, what will you give me if I do?"

"You can have my jewels, my finest clothes and even my crown if you will find my ball," said the princess hastily, for she was truly eager to get her favourite toy back.

"I do not want your jewels, your clothes or your crown," replied the frog. "I would like to be your friend. I want to return with you to the palace and eat from your golden plate and sip from your golden cup. At night I want to sleep on a cushion made of silk next to your bed and I want you to kiss me goodnight before I go to sleep, too."

"I promise all you ask," said the girl, "if only you will find my golden ball."

"Remember what you have promised," said the frog, as he dived deep into the pond. At last he surfaced again with the ball and threw it on to the grass beside the princess. She was so overjoyed she forgot all about thanking the frog – let alone her promise – and ran all the way back to the palace.

That evening the king, the queen and the princess were having dinner in the great hall of the palace, when a courtier approached the king and said, "Your majesty, there is a frog at the door who says the princess has promised to share her dinner with him."

"Is this true?" demanded the king, turning to the princess and looking rather angry.

"Yes, it is," said the princess in a small voice. And she told her father the whole story.

"When a promise is made it must be kept, my girl," said the king. "You must ask the frog to dine with you."

Presently, the frog hopped into the great hall and round to where the princess was sitting. With a great leap he was up on the table beside her. She stifled a scream.

"You promised to let me eat from your golden plate," said the frog, tucking into the princess's food. The princess felt quite sick and pushed the plate away from her. Then to her horror the frog dipped his long tongue into her golden cup and drank every drop. "It's what you promised," he reminded her.

When he had finished, the frog stretched his long, green limbs, yawned and said, "Now I feel quite sleepy. Please take me to your room."

"Do I have to?" the princess pleaded with her father.

"Yes, you do," said the king sternly. "The frog helped you when you were in need and you made him a promise."

So the princess carried the frog to her bedroom but as they reached the door she said, "My bedroom's very warm. I'm sure you'd be more comfortable out here where it's cool."

But as she opened the bedroom door, the frog leaped from her hand and landed on her bed.

"You promised that I could sleep on a silk cushion next to your bed," said the frog.

"Yes, yes, of course," said the princess looking with horror at the froggy footprints on her clean, white sheets. She called to her maid to bring a cushion.

The frog jumped on to the cushion and looked as though he was going to sleep.

"Good," thought the princess, "he's forgotten about my final promise."

But just as she was about to get into bed, he opened his eyes and said, "What about my goodnight kiss?"

"Oh, woe is me," thought the princess as she closed her eyes and pursed her lips towards the frog's cold and clammy face and kissed him.

"Open your eyes," said a voice that didn't sound a bit like the frog's. She opened her eyes and there, standing before her, was a prince. The princess stood there in dumbstruck amazement.

"Thank you," said the prince. "You have broken a spell cast upon me by a wicked witch. She turned me into a frog and said the spell would only be broken if a princess would eat with me, sleep beside me and kiss me."

They ran to tell the king what had happened. He was delighted and said, "You may live in the palace from now on, for my daughter needs a friend." And indeed, the prince and princess became the best of friends and she was never lonely again. He taught her to play football with the golden ball and she taught him to ride her pony. One day, many years later, they were married and had lots of children. And, do you know, their children were particularly good at leapfrog.

Goldilocks and the Three Bears

There once lived a little girl who had long, golden hair. Because of this, everyone knew her as Goldilocks. Goldilocks and her mother lived together in a cosy little cottage in the forest.

"Would you like some pretty flowers?" Goldilocks asked her mother one day. "I will pick you some if you like."

"That would be lovely, my dear," said her mother. "But mind you don't get lost. Don't stray too far, and don't be too long."

Goldilocks gave her mother a big hug and promised to be careful. She picked up her little flower basket and skipped off into the forest to look for flowers.

First she came upon some big, bright daffodils. She picked a few and placed them in her basket. A little further on, she spied some pretty bluebells and so she picked a bunch of those as well. Then she saw, even further on, some lovely marigolds which she also picked and put into her basket.

Well, Goldilocks was so busy picking all these wonderful flowers that she wandered further and further into the forest. Suddenly she realised that she was lost. She didn't know which way to turn. She was also beginning to feel very hungry and tired.

Just when she was wondering what to do next, she saw a small cottage nestling among the trees. She went up to it and looked through the windows, but couldn't see anyone inside. But the door was open and so she went in. Inside the cottage she found a table laid out with three bowls of steaming porridge. There was a big bowl, a medium-sized bowl and a little bowl. The table also had three chairs arranged around it, one next to each of the bowls of porridge. There was a big chair, a medium-sized chair and a little chair.

54

Goldilocks was so tired that she simply had to sit down. First she sat down in the big chair, but it was very hard and lumpy. It wasn't comfortable at all. Then she tried the medium-sized chair, but that didn't feel comfortable either. At last, she tried the little chair, but as soon as she sat down in it – it broke! She was too heavy for the little chair. "Oh dear," thought Goldilocks.

Instead of sitting down, she thought she would have some porridge as she was still very hungry. First she took a spoonful of porridge from the big bowl. But it was too hot, and so she couldn't eat it. Then she tried a spoonful from the medium-sized bowl, but it was too lumpy. So she tried a spoonful from the little bowl. And guess what? It tasted so delicious that she ate it all up!

55

"Oh, I do feel sleepy," yawned Goldilocks after she had finished the porridge in the little bowl. "I wonder if there is a nice, comfortable bed I can sleep in."

So she went upstairs and found a bedroom with three beds in it. There was a big bed, a medium-sized bed and a little bed. First she tried the big bed, but it was very hard and didn't feel comfortable at all. Next she tried the medium-sized bed, but it was too soft and that didn't feel comfortable either. Finally, she tried the little bed. It was just right – warm and cosy. Soon she was fast asleep.

Just then, the family of three bears who lived in the cottage came back from their walk in the forest. As soon as they came in through the front door, they knew someone had been there.

"Who has been sitting in
my chair?" said Daddy Bear,
in a deep, gruff voice.

"And who has been
sitting in my chair?"
asked Mummy Bear
in a softer voice.

"Who has broken
my chair?" cried Baby
Bear in a squeaky voice.

Then the three bears looked on the table.

"Someone has been trying my porridge," said Daddy Bear.

"And someone has been trying my porridge, too," said Mummy Bear.

"Who has eaten all my porridge?" said Baby Bear, who by now was very upset and sobbing big tears.

Upstairs went the three bears and into their bedroom.

"Who has been sleeping in my bed?" asked Daddy Bear.

"And who has been sleeping in my bed?" asked Mummy Bear.

Suddenly, Baby Bear gave a cry of surprise. "Look!" he yelled.

"There's someone sleeping in my bed."

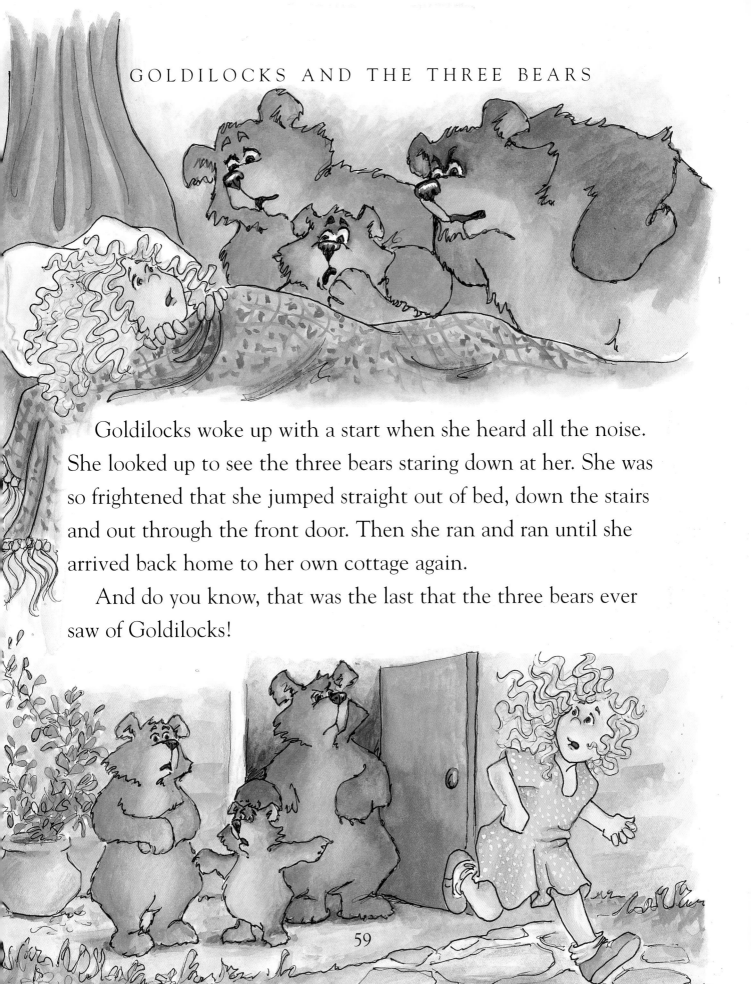

Goldilocks woke up with a start when she heard all the noise. She looked up to see the three bears staring down at her. She was so frightened that she jumped straight out of bed, down the stairs and out through the front door. Then she ran and ran until she arrived back home to her own cottage again.

And do you know, that was the last that the three bears ever saw of Goldilocks!

The Lost Lion

Once there was a lion cub called Lenny. He was a very tiny lion
cub, but he was sure that he was the bravest lion in all of Africa.
When his mother taught her cubs how to stalk prey, Lenny
would stalk his own mother and pounce on her. When she
showed them how to wash themselves, Lenny licked his sister's
face instead so that she growled at him. When the mother
lioness led her cubs down to the watering hole to drink, he
jumped into the water and created a huge splash that soaked
everyone.

The other lionesses were not amused. "You'd better watch
that son of yours," they said to Lenny's mother, "or he'll get
into really big trouble."

One day the mother lioness led her
cubs on their first big hunt. "Stay close to me,"
she said, "or you could get hurt."
She crawled off through the undergrowth with
her cubs following on behind, one after the other. Lenny was at
the back. The grass tickled his tummy and he wanted to laugh,
but he was trying hard to be obedient. So he crawled along,
making sure he kept the bobbing tail of the cub in front in sight.
On and on they crawled until Lenny was beginning to feel quite
weary.

"But a brave lion cub doesn't give up," he thought to himself.
And on he plodded.

At last the grass gave way to a clearing. Lenny looked up, and to
his dismay he saw that the tail he had been following was attached,
not to one of his brothers or sisters, but to a baby elephant!

Somewhere along the trail he had started following the wrong tail and now he was hopelessly lost. He wanted to cry out for his mother but then he remembered that he was the bravest lion in all of Africa. So what do you think he did? He went straight up to the mother elephant and growled his fiercest growl at her. "That'll frighten her!" thought Lenny. "She won't dare growl back!" And, of course, she didn't growl back. Instead she lifted her trunk and trumpeted so loudly at Lenny that he was blown off his feet and through the air and landed against the hard trunk of a tree.

Lenny got up and found that his knees were knocking. "Oh my," he thought, "that elephant has a very loud growl. But I'm still definitely the bravest lion in all of Africa." He set off across the plain. It was getting hot in the midday sun and soon Lenny began to feel sleepy. "I think I'll just take a nap in that tree," he thought, and started climbing up into the branches.

To his surprise, he found that the tree was already occupied by a large leopard. "I'll show him who's boss," thought Lenny, baring his tiny claws. The leopard raised his head to look at Lenny, and then bared his own huge, razor-sharp claws. He took a swipe at Lenny with his paw. Without even touching Lenny, the wind from the leopard's great paw swept Lenny out of the tree and he landed with a bump on the ground.

Lenny got up and found that his legs were trembling. "Oh my," he thought, "that leopard had big claws. But I'm still definitely the bravest lion in Africa." He set off again across the plain. After a while he began to feel quite hungry. "I wonder what I can find to eat," he thought. Just then he saw a spotted shape lying low in the grass. "That looks like a tasty meal," thought Lenny as he pounced on the spotted shape.

63

But the spotted shape was a cheetah! Quick as a flash, the cheetah sprang away and as he did so, his tail caught Lenny a blow that sent him spinning round and round in circles.

 When Lenny stopped spinning, he got up and found that his whole body was shaking. "Oh my," he thought, "that cheetah is a fast runner." Then he added in rather a small voice, "But I'm still the bravest lion in Africa." He set off again across the plain. By now it was getting dark and Lenny was wishing he was at home with his mother and brothers and sisters. "I wonder if they've noticed I've gone," he thought sadly as a tear rolled down his furry cheek. He felt cold and tired and hungry as he crawled into the undergrowth to sleep.

 Some time later Lenny was woken by a noise that was louder than anything he'd ever heard before – louder even than the elephant's trumpeting. It filled the night air and made the leaves on the trees shake. The noise was getting louder and louder and

the animal that was making it was getting nearer and nearer. Lenny peeped out from his hiding place and saw a huge golden creature with big yellow eyes that shone in the dark like lamps. It had a great crown of shaggy golden fur all around its head and its red jaws were open wide revealing a set of very large white fangs. How it roared! Lenny was terrified and about to turn tail and run, when the animal stopped roaring and spoke to him. "Come here, Lenny," said the animal gently. "It's me, your father, and I'm going to take you home. Climb up on my back, little one."

So Lenny climbed up on his father's back and was carried all the way home. And when they got there his father told his mother and his brothers and sisters that Lenny had been a very brave lion after all.

Snow White

In the middle of winter, a young queen sat sewing by an open window. As she looked up and saw the snow falling, she pricked her finger and three drops of blood fell on to the snow. The red of the blood on the white snow, framed by the black ebony window frame, was so striking that the queen made a wish that she could have a child that was as red as blood, as white as snow and as black as ebony.

In time the queen's wish came true. She gave birth to a baby girl with snow-white skin, blood-red lips and hair as black as ebony. The young queen died soon after the child was born, and the king named his daughter Snow White. Soon the king took a second wife, as beautiful as the first. But this one was also vain. She had a magic mirror and sometimes she stood in front of it and said, "Mirror, mirror, on the wall, who is the fairest of them all?"

And the mirror answered, "You are the fairest one of all."

Then the queen was happy because she knew that the mirror always told the truth.

Years passed and Snow White grew more and more beautiful. One day the queen stood in front of the mirror and asked, "Mirror, mirror, on the wall, who is the fairest of them all?"

And the mirror answered, "You were the fairest one, 'tis true, but now Snow White is lovelier than you."

From that moment on, the queen began to hate Snow White. She couldn't rest until she was rid of the girl, so she called her huntsman and said, "Take Snow White into the forest and kill her. And bring back her heart."

The huntsman could not bear to kill the little girl. He told Snow White to run away into the woods. "She won't survive for long without food and shelter," thought the huntsman with remorse. To satisfy the queen, he shot a wild boar and took back its heart.

Snow White went deeper into the woods until she was completely lost. At last she came to a house. Inside was a table with a white cloth laid for seven people, with food and drink at every place. Along one wall were seven beds covered with white quilts. Snow White was so hungry that she took a mouthful from each plate and a sip from each cup. Then she tried out all the beds but they were all too long, or too short, or too wide or too narrow – until she came to the last one of all, which was just right. She lay down and fell fast asleep. Some time later the owners of the house returned. They were seven dwarfs who worked all day mining gold in the mountains. They could soon tell that they had received a visitor.

"Someone's been sitting in my chair," said the first dwarf.

"And eating my food," said the second.

"And drinking my wine," said the third.

"And using my knife," said the fourth.

"And my fork," said the fifth.

"And my spoon," said the sixth.

"And she's asleep on my bed!" said the seventh dwarf.

The dwarfs all crowded around Snow White. She looked so comfortable that they let her sleep in peace.

In the morning, when Snow White woke up, she was frightened at first, but the dwarfs reassured her. She told them what had happened. "You can stay with us," they said. "You can clean our house, cook and wash for us and we will protect you." So Snow White stayed with the dwarfs. Each day when they went off to work they reminded her, "Don't let anyone in." And Snow White promised that she wouldn't.

For a while the queen felt happy again now that she thought Snow White was dead. Then one day, she stood in front of the mirror again and asked, "Mirror, mirror, on the wall, who is the fairest of them all?"

And the mirror answered, "Over the hills where the seven dwarfs dwell, Snow White is still alive and well. And though you are fairer than most, 'tis true, she is still far lovelier than you."

The queen was furious. "This time I'll finish her off myself," she screeched. Disguising herself as a pedlar she made the journey to the dwarfs' house. "Silks for sale. Ribbons and laces," she called.

Snow White looked out of the window and saw the fine things. "Surely it wouldn't hurt to look," she thought. She unlocked the door and chose a pretty lace.

"Let me thread it for you," offered the old woman. Then she laced Snow White's bodice so tightly that the girl couldn't breathe and she fell to the floor unconscious.

When the dwarfs returned that night, they found her and cut the laces. Snow White began to breathe again and soon she was able to tell them what had happened. "That was the queen," they told her, "and she'll be back."

For a while all was well, then again the queen stood in front of her mirror and asked, "Mirror, mirror, on the wall, who is the fairest of them all?"

And again the mirror answered, "Over the hills where the seven dwarfs dwell, Snow White is still alive and well. And though you are fairer than most, 'tis true, she is still far lovelier than you."

The queen was furious. This time she prepared a poisoned comb and set off for the dwarfs' house in a different disguise. "Come and buy my lovely combs," she called. This time Snow White refused to open the door. "Let me pass you one through the window," said the queen.

"Well there's no harm in that," thought Snow White, undoing the latch.

The queen leaned through the window. "Let me comb your lovely hair with this fine comb," she said. As soon as the comb touched Snow White's head, the poison began to work and she fell senseless to the ground.

The dwarfs came home to find Snow White lying on the floor. Carefully they removed the comb and she returned to life. Meanwhile, the queen returned to the castle and immediately went up to the mirror and repeated her question. Imagine her anger when she got the same reply as before. Now she prepared a special apple. One side was green, while the other was red. The queen poisoned the red half, then she set off for the dwarfs' house once more. This time she pretended to be a farmer's wife. Once again Snow White refused to open the door. "Don't worry," said the queen. "Have an apple anyway." She held out the poisoned apple.

"No, no, I mustn't," said Snow White, though the apple did look very tasty.

"Tell you what," said the queen, "we'll have half each."

"Well, it can't be poisoned," thought Snow White.

The queen carefully cut the apple in half. "Here, I'll have the sour green half and you have the nice sweet red half," she said. Snow White took the apple, but the moment she bit into it she fell down dead.

72

SNOW WHITE

The queen hurried back to the castle and this time when she spoke to the mirror it replied, to her pleasure, "You are the fairest one of all."

The dwarfs came home and found Snow White. They wept bitterly when they saw that she was dead. They placed her in a glass coffin and set it on a hillside and took turns to guard her. One day a prince came upon the coffin. He was so moved by Snow White that he asked the dwarfs if he could take her with him. He was heartbroken when the dwarfs refused. In the end, they took pity upon him and agreed. As the prince's servants lifted the coffin, one of them stumbled. The apple dislodged itself from her throat and Snow White came back to life.

The prince asked Snow White to marry him and when she agreed, everyone was invited to the wedding, and nothing more was ever heard of the wicked queen.

The Magic Tree

Tommy rubbed his eyes, blinked hard, and looked out of his bedroom window again. But it was still there – an enormous oak tree that definitely hadn't been there yesterday! If it had been there, he'd have known all about it for sure. For a start he would have climbed up it, for Tommy loved nothing better than climbing trees.

No, this tree was definitely not there yesterday! Tommy sat staring at the tree in wonder and disbelief. The tree stood there, outside his bedroom window, with its huge, spreading branches almost asking to be climbed. Tommy wondered how on earth it had suddenly got there, but he decided that before he wondered about that too much, he had better go and climb it first. After all, there was always time later to wonder about things but never enough time to do things, he thought.

As soon as he was dressed, he ran outside to take a closer look at the new tree. It seemed just like any other big oak tree. It had lots of wide, inviting branches and lots of green, rounded leaves. And it had deep, furrowed bark just like any other oak tree.

Tommy couldn't resist any longer. On to the lowest branch he stepped and then up to the next. The tree seemed so easy to climb. There were branches everywhere. In no time at all, he was in a green, leafy canopy. He couldn't even see the ground any more. But something seemed not quite right. The branches beneath his feet seemed to be so big now that he could stand up on them and walk in any direction. And the branches all around him seemed just like trees themselves. In fact, he suddenly realised that he wasn't any longer climbing a tree, but standing in a whole forest full of trees.

Tommy didn't like this at all, and thought he had better get down. But where was down? All he could see were tall, swaying trees and here and there a twisty path leading off even deeper into the forest. Tommy didn't know how he had done it, but he had somehow got himself completely lost in a forest, and he hadn't even had breakfast yet!

Worse still, it seemed to be getting dark. "Quick, over here!" a voice suddenly called out. Tommy was very startled, but he was even more startled when he saw that the voice belonged to a squirrel.

"You can speak!" blurted out Tommy.

"Of course I can speak!" snapped the squirrel. "Now listen. You are in great danger, and there's no time to lose if we are to save you from the clutches of the evil Wizard of the Woods."

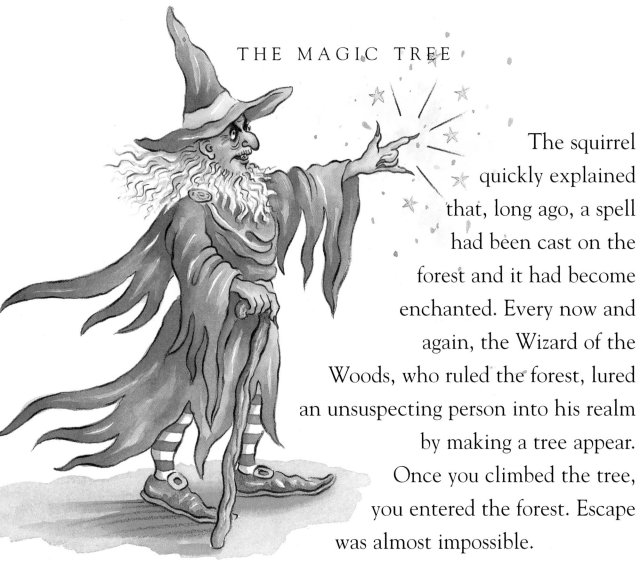

The squirrel quickly explained that, long ago, a spell had been cast on the forest and it had become enchanted. Every now and again, the Wizard of the Woods, who ruled the forest, lured an unsuspecting person into his realm by making a tree appear. Once you climbed the tree, you entered the forest. Escape was almost impossible.

"But why does the Wizard of the Woods want to lure people into the forest?" asked Tommy, rather hoping that he didn't have to hear the answer.

"To turn them into fertilizer to make the trees grow," said the squirrel.

Tommy didn't really know what fertilizer was, but it sounded rather nasty. He was pleased when the squirrel suddenly said, "There is just one way to get you out of here. But we must hurry. Soon it will be dark and the Wizard of the Woods will awake. Once he awakes, he will smell your blood and he will capture you."

With that, the squirrel jumped up the nearest tree. "Follow me," he said.

Tommy immediately climbed after the squirrel. "Where are we going?" he panted as they climbed higher and higher.

"To the top of the tallest tree in the forest," the squirrel answered as they clambered from tree to tree, climbing ever higher.

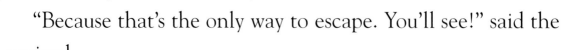"But why?" asked Tommy.

"Because that's the only way to escape. You'll see!" said the squirrel.

Eventually they stopped climbing. They were at the top of the tallest tree in the forest. Below them and around them was nothing but more trees. Tommy looked up, and at last he could see the clear, twilight sky. He also noticed something rather strange. All the leaves at the top of the tallest tree were enormous.

"Quick, time is running out," said the squirrel. "Sit on this leaf and hold tight."

Tommy sat on one of the huge leaves. The squirrel whistled, and before Tommy could blink he had been joined by a hundred more squirrels. They each took hold of the branch to which the leaf was attached. With a great heave, they pulled and pulled until the branch was bent backwards. Suddenly they let go. With a mighty "TWANG", the branch, with Tommy and the leaf attached, sprang forward. As it did so Tommy and the leaf were launched into the air. High above the trees they soared until, ever so slowly, they began to float down to earth. Down, down, they went, until they landed with a bump.

Tommy opened his eyes to find himself on his bedroom floor. He ran over to the window and looked out. The magic tree was nowhere to be seen. It had gone as quickly as it had appeared. But perhaps it had never been there at all. Maybe it was just a dream. What do you think?

The Invisible Imp

One day, Sarah Jones was pegging out her washing. It was a lovely day and she was looking forward to visiting her friend Rose. "I'll just get this washing on the line while the sun's shining," she said to herself, "and then I'll be on my way."

After a while, she stopped and looked down into the basket. "That's very peculiar!" she thought. "I know I've already pegged out that green shirt and there it is back in the basket." She carried on pegging out the clothes. Now she shook her head in disbelief. For although she had been working away for quite a while, the basket of washing was still full and there was almost nothing on the line! She began to get quite cross, for she was going to be late getting to Rose's house.

Try as she might, she just could not get that washing pegged. In the end, she had to leave the basket of wet washing and run to Rose's house.

"I'm so sorry I'm late, Rose," she gasped, all out of breath from running. Sarah told Rose all about what had happened.

"Well," said Rose, "that's a strange coincidence. I was baking some cakes for us to have for tea. Every time I put them in the oven and turned away, they were out of the oven and on the table again! In the end I had to stand guard over them – which reminds me, they were just beginning to cook nicely when you knocked on the door."

The two women went into Rose's kitchen and there were the cakes, sitting on the table again, half-cooked. "Now they're ruined!" cried Rose. "Whatever shall we do?"

81

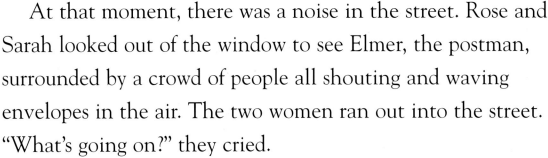

At that moment, there was a noise in the street. Rose and Sarah looked out of the window to see Elmer, the postman, surrounded by a crowd of people all shouting and waving envelopes in the air. The two women ran out into the street. "What's going on?" they cried.

"Elmer's given us all the wrong post," said Rose's neighbour, Dora. "He's normally so reliable, but this morning he seems to have gone completely crazy. Now we've got to sort out all the mail for him."

"I don't know what's happened," wailed Elmer in anguish. "I'm sure I posted all the letters through the right doors."

"Well," said Sarah, "Rose and I have also found strange things happening to us this morning." She told the crowd their stories. Everyone forgave Elmer when they realised it wasn't his fault, but they were still truly mystified as to what – or who – could have caused all these problems.

But that wasn't the end of it. Oh no, indeed! The butcher's wife served her family mutton stew, but when she lifted the lid the family heard a bleating sound and a little lamb leaped out of the pot. The milkman delivered the milk as usual, but when people took their milk indoors, they found the bottles were full of lemonade. Old Mr Smith tried to pull his chair up to the table and found it was stuck hard to the floor. And when Mrs Smith painted her bedroom blue, she came back and found it had changed to pink with purple spots.

Can you guess what had happened? Do you know who'd been up to all these tricks? It was an imp, of course! The wicked little fellow had become bored playing pranks on the fairies and goblins in fairyland. By now, they knew all his tricks and he was finding it harder and harder to catch them out. Then he had an idea. Why not play tricks in the human world where he would be invisible? So that's exactly what he did.

At first, he really only meant
to play one or two tricks, but he
had such fun that he couldn't
resist carrying on.

Well, the invisible imp continued
on with his tricks. But of course, as you know,
pride comes before a fall, and one day he just went too far. Sarah
Jones had been invited to a party. It was to be a fancy dress party
and on the invitation it said: "*Please wear red*". Now Sarah
fretted because she had no red clothes at all. Then she
had an idea. She got out an old blue frock from the
back of the cupboard. "I'll dye it red," she thought.

She mixed a big tub of red dye and was just about to put the
dress into it, when along came the invisible imp. "Here's some
fun!" he thought. "I'll turn the dye blue. Then she won't know
why her dress hasn't changed colour. Won't that be funny!" And
he started giggling to himself at the thought of it. He danced up
and down on the edge of the tub, thinking up
a really evil spell to turn the dye blue.

But he laughed so much to himself
that he slipped and fell right into
the bright red mixture. Fast as
lightning out he scrambled
and cast his spell.

84

Sure enough Sarah fished out the dress from the tub, and to her dismay saw that it was exactly the same colour as when she had put it into the dye. She was about to peer into the tub when something caught her eye. For there, sitting on the table, chuckling to himself and holding his sides with laughter, was a bright red imp. And there was a trail of tiny red footprints from the tub of dye to the table. The silly imp had no idea that he was no longer invisible and that Sarah could see him as plain as the nose on her face! In a flash Sarah realised what had happened. She chased the imp out of the house and down the street and, I'm glad to say, he wasn't able to play his mischievous tricks ever again.

Ursula's Umbrella

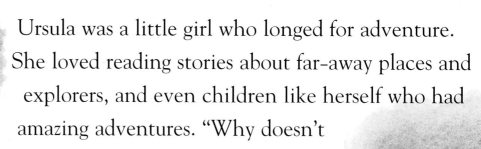

Ursula was a little girl who longed for adventure. She loved reading stories about far-away places and explorers, and even children like herself who had amazing adventures. "Why doesn't anything interesting ever happen to me?" she sighed. "How I wish I could fly to the moon or dive to the deepest part of the ocean. What fun it would be!"

One windy day, Ursula went out for a walk. She took her umbrella with her because it looked as though it might be going to rain. Ursula's umbrella was red with a shiny black handle. It was also very large indeed. People used to laugh as Ursula walked along the street with her umbrella up. It looked so big and Ursula was so small that it seemed as though the umbrella was walking along all by itself!

URSULA'S UMBRELLA

As Ursula walked up the street she felt a few raindrops on her nose. "Better put up my umbrella," she thought. She unfurled her umbrella and lifted it up above her head. As she did so, a great gust of wind came and swept her right off the pavement. It carried her past the upstairs windows of the houses, past the roofs and the chimney pots and up, up, into the sky. Ursula clung tightly to the umbrella handle. She was surprised to find she didn't feel the least bit frightened. No, not a bit. She felt very excited. She looked down and saw streets and factories whizzing past far below. Then she saw fields and something that looked like a silver thread snaking through the countryside. "A river!" thought Ursula.

Now she could see the coastline, and soon the umbrella was carrying her out over the ocean. At first when she looked down the sea was grey, but gradually it turned to the deepest blue with frothy white waves. "How I'd love a swim," thought Ursula. At that moment she felt the umbrella starting to descend. Looking down she could see that they were heading for an island in the middle of the ocean. Soon she was floating past the tops of palm trees and, as she touched the ground, she felt sand under her feet.

"I'm going for a swim!" said Ursula to herself. She folded up her umbrella and set off to the beach. The water felt deliciously warm as Ursula paddled about. She looked down and saw that the water was amazingly clear. She could see brightly coloured fish darting in and out of the coral. "Wow!" exclaimed Ursula out loud and then "Wow!" again, though this time much louder as she looked up and saw a black fin skimming through the water towards her. "Shark!" she shrieked, but no-one heard.

Then all of a sudden a gust of wind made her umbrella unfurl itself and float towards her in the water, like a boat.

Ursula made a dash for the umbrella, hurled herself into it and floated away across the sea. "That was quite an adventure!" she thought.

After a while, Ursula looked out over the rim of the umbrella and saw that it was heading for the shore again. This time, when Ursula stepped out of the umbrella, she found that she was at the edge of a jungle. Folding up the umbrella, she set off into the forest. She followed an overgrown path through the trees. "I wonder where this leads?" thought Ursula. She wiped her brow and swatted the insects that flew in front of her face. Deeper and deeper into the jungle she went.

Suddenly she heard the sound of rushing water and found herself standing on the banks of a river. All at once she heard another sound. It was the crashing noise of some enormous beast approaching through the trees.

Where could she run to? Suddenly she felt the umbrella being blown from her hand. To her amazement it fell to the ground, stretching right across the river like a bridge. Ursula walked over to the other side, not daring to look down at the torrent below. When she was safely on the far bank she looked back to see a large puma, with glittering green eyes, glaring at her from the opposite bank. "That was a lucky escape!" thought Ursula.

Ursula could see a mountain through the trees and decided to head towards it. "I'll be able to get a good view from the top and maybe find my way home," she thought. She struggled on through the forest and eventually found herself at the foot of the mountain. There seemed to be no way up the sheer rock face.

Ursula was on the point of despair when suddenly another great gust of wind blew up. It carried Ursula, clinging to her opened umbrella, all the way up to the top of the mountain.

90

URSULA'S UMBRELLA

At the top of the mountain, the umbrella let her gently down again and her feet landed in deep snow. By now it was blowing a blizzard and she could not see anything except white snowflakes in all directions. "There's only one thing to do," thought Ursula. She put the umbrella on the snow, sat on it and whizzed all the way down the other side of the mountain.

When she reached the bottom, to her surprise, the umbrella sledge didn't stop but carried on through the snowstorm until eventually, after a very long time, it came to a halt right outside her own front door. "Well, that was quite an adventure," said Ursula, shaking the snow off the umbrella, before folding it up.

She stepped inside the front door. "Wherever have you been?" said her mother. "You look as though you've been to the ends of the Earth and back."

"Well I have," Ursula was about to say. But then she thought that no-one would believe her and it was nicer to keep her adventures to herself. And that is what she did.

Esmerelda the Ragdoll

At the back of the toy cupboard on a dark and dusty shelf lay Esmerelda the ragdoll. She lay on her back and stared at the shelf above, as she had done for a very long time. It seemed to Esmerelda that it was many years since she had been lifted up by Clara, her owner, and even longer since she had been out in the playroom with the other toys. Now her lovely yellow hair was all tangled and her beautiful blue dress was creased, torn and faded. Each time Clara opened the toy cupboard door, Esmerelda hoped very much that she would be chosen, but Clara always played with the newer toys at the front of the cupboard. Every time Clara put her toys back in the cupboard, Esmerelda felt herself being pushed further towards the back. It was very uncomfortable and indeed, Esmerelda might have suffocated if it wasn't for a hole at the back of the cupboard, which enabled her to breathe.

These days Esmerelda felt very lonely. Until recently a one-eyed teddy bear had been beside her on the shelf. Then one day he had fallen through the hole at the back of the cupboard and was never seen again. Esmerelda missed him dreadfully, for he had been a lovely old teddy with a gentle nature. Now she, too, could feel herself being pushed towards the hole. She felt a mixture of excitement and fright at the prospect of falling through it. Sometimes she imagined that she would land on a soft feather bed belonging to a little girl who would really love her. At other times she thought that the hole led to a terrifying land full of monsters.

One day Esmerelda heard Clara's mother say, "Now Clara, today you must tidy up the toy cupboard and clear out all those old toys you no longer play with."

Esmerelda could see Clara's small hands reaching into the cupboard. She couldn't bear the thought of being picked up by the little girl and then discarded. "There's only one thing to do," she said to herself. She wriggled towards the hole, closed her eyes and jumped. Esmerelda felt herself falling, and then she landed with a bump on something soft.

"Watch out, my dear!" said a familiar voice from underneath her. Esmerelda opened her eyes and saw that she had landed on One-eyed Ted.

The two toys were so overjoyed to see each other again that they hugged one another. "What shall we do now?" cried Esmerelda.

"I have an idea," said Ted. "There's a rusty old toy car over there. I wanted to escape in it, but I can't drive with only one eye. What do you think? Shall we give it a go?"

"Yes, yes!" exclaimed Esmerelda, climbing into the driver's seat.

By now One-eyed Ted had found the key and was winding up the car. "Away we go!" he called as they sped off.

"Where are we going?" shouted Esmerelda.

"To the seaside," replied Ted.

"Which way is it?" asked Esmerelda, holding on to her yellow hair streaming behind her in the wind.

"I don't know. We'll have to ask the way," said Ted.

Rounding a bend, they came across a black cat crossing the road. "Excuse me," called Ted, "could you tell us the way to the seaside?"

Now, as you know, cats hate water. "Whatever do they want to go near water for? Why should I help them?" thought the cat. "It's the other side of that mountain," he growled as he ran off.

On sped the rusty car, and up the mountainside. When they reached the top of the mountain they met a sheep. Now, as you know, sheep never listen properly. "Excuse me," said Esmerelda, "where can we find the beach?"

Well, the silly sheep thought Esmerelda was asking where they could find a peach! "Down there," she bleated, nodding towards an orchard in the valley below.

Esmerelda and Ted leaped back into the car and sped off down the mountainside, but when they reached the orchard there was no sign of water, of course – just a lot of peach trees.

95

Once again they scratched their heads in
puzzlement. Just then a mole popped his head out
of the earth. "Excuse me," said Ted, "would
you happen to know how we can
find the seaside?"

Now the mole was very wise, but
unfortunately he was also, as you know, very short sighted. He
peered at Esmerelda's blue dress. "That patch of blue must surely
be a river, and rivers run into the sea," he thought.

"Just follow that river," he said, "and you'll end up at the seaside.
Good day!" And with that he disappeared under ground again.

Esmerelda and Ted looked even more puzzled, for there was
no sign of a river in the orchard. "Oh well," sighed Esmerelda,
"perhaps we'll never find the seaside."

"Don't give up," said Ted. "We'll surely find it in the end." They
climbed back in the rusty car and set off again. After a short while
the car started to splutter and then it came to a complete halt at
the side of the road. "What shall we do now?" cried Esmerelda.

"We'll just have to wait here and see what happens," said Ted.
It seemed like a very long time that they sat beside the road. At
long last they heard footsteps, and then Esmerelda felt herself
being picked up.

"Look – it's a dear old tatty ragdoll," said a voice. Esmerelda
looked up and saw that she was being carried by a little girl.

Ted and the rusty car had been picked up by the girl's father. "We'll take them home and look after them," the man said.

Now they were in a real car and before long the toys found themselves in a house. The little girl carried Esmerelda, One-eyed Ted and the rusty car upstairs to her bedroom and put them down on a window sill. "I'll be back soon," she whispered.

Esmerelda looked out of the window and nearly danced for joy. "Look, look Ted," she shouted. For out of the window she could see the road, and beyond the road was a beach and then the sea. "We reached the seaside after all," she cried.

Esmerelda, Ted and the rusty car lived happily in the house beside the sea. Esmerelda's hair was brushed and plaited and she was given a beautiful new dress. Ted had a new eye sewn on and could see properly again. The rusty car was painted and oiled. Most days the little girl took her new toys down to the beach to play with, and the days in the dark toy cupboard were soon forgotten. The little girl used to tell her friends the story of how she had found her three best toys lying beside the road one day. And as for the toys, well, they sometimes talked about that strange day when they had such an adventure – and they'd burst out laughing.

Cinderella

Once upon a time there was a beautiful young girl who lived
with her widowed father. He had brought her up to be kind and
gentle. All went well until the day the girl's father married again.
His second wife was very proud of her house. Everything always
had to be spotlessly clean. Worse than that, she had two spiteful
daughters. All three had terrible tempers, and they hated the
beautiful young girl with a vengeance. All day long from dawn to
dusk she was made to scrub and clean, mend clothes and serve at
the table. At night, while the household slept, there was coal to
fetch, fires to be laid and the table to be set for breakfast the
following day.

The stepmother gave her own two daughters the finest rooms in the house. To her stepdaughter, she gave the coldest attic room, with the hardest bed and a quilt cover that was so thin it barely kept out the winter chill. To keep warm, the poor girl had to sit in the chimney nook of the kitchen with her feet near the cinders. Because of this, her stepsisters nicknamed her Cinderella.

One day a footman called at the house to deliver an invitation. Cinderella carried it into the dining room where her stepsisters were having breakfast. "What have you there?" shrieked one of them, snatching the envelope from her hand. She tore it open with her long, polished nails. "Ooh!" she cried. "It's an invitation from the prince to attend a ball tomorrow night!"

The other sister jumped up and down with delight. "We're going to a ball!" she yelled.

"Am I invited, too?" asked Cinderella shyly.

"You?" cried the elder sister.

"You – invited to the palace ball?" cried the other sister, and they both burst into fits of laughter. The elder sister, who was very plump, laughed so much that she became quite breathless and had to ask Cinderella to loosen her corset.

The sisters spent the next day preparing for the ball. Cinderella was kept very busy, pressing and starching the girls' ballgowns, curling their hair and fixing bows and ribbons. They told her to lace their corsets extra tight to make them look slimmer. She was made to run hither and thither all day. "Fetch my pearl necklace!" called one.

"Polish my party shoes!" demanded the other. At last both sisters were ready to go, and set off by carriage to the ball. "Don't wait up!" they shouted out of the window to Cinderella, as the coach sped away.

Cinderella went back into the kitchen. Now the house seemed calm and quiet at last. She picked up a broom and danced slowly round the room, imagining that she was at the ball. "How wonderful it would be to go to the ball," she sighed wistfully, and sat down by the fire where it was warm and started to cry.

"Don't cry, my child," said a gentle voice.

Cinderella looked up to see a beautiful stranger standing before her. "Who are you?" said Cinderella.

"I am your fairy godmother," came the reply. "Now, dry your tears. Would you like to go to the ball?" said the fairy.

"Oh, yes please," cried Cinderella, leaping up.

"Then you shall go," said the fairy. "But first, run into the garden, and fetch me a nice fat pumpkin." Cinderella did as she was told. When she returned, the fairy godmother tapped the pumpkin with her magic wand and instantly it was transformed into a sparkling glass coach.

"Now we need some horses," said the fairy. At that moment there was a scuttling noise in the corner of the kitchen and four white mice popped out of a hole. In an instant the fairy godmother tapped them with her wand and they became four handsome white horses. "Now what about a footman," she said. Before Cinderella could speak she tapped Cinderella's black cat and there before her very eyes stood a footman. "Now there's just one more thing we need before you go," said the fairy, "and that's a coachman."

Cinderella looked about the kitchen and scratched her head.

Then she ran into the garden and came back with a live frog. "Will he do?" she asked her fairy godmother.

"Indeed he will," replied the fairy, tapping the frog. And suddenly there was a coachman standing by the coach.

"All aboard!" he cried.

Cinderella was just about to leap inside when her godmother called her back. "I nearly forgot something," she said.

The tip of her wand touched Cinderella's ragged clothes and Cinderella looked down to see, to her astonishment, that she was wearing the most beautiful ballgown that there ever was. At her neck glittered a diamond necklace and on her feet were a dainty pair of glass slippers. "Have a lovely time at the ball," said her godmother. "But do not stay a minute longer than midnight, for on the stroke of twelve, everything will be as it was before."

And with that, she vanished.

When Cinderella arrived at the ball, she found herself in a dazzling ballroom filled with people. Everyone stopped to stare at this beautiful girl, and soon the prince himself approached and asked her to dance. "Who is she?" people were asking. The prince and Cinderella danced together all evening. Her stepsisters watched, never once guessing who she was.

"Isn't she beautiful," remarked the elder sister jealously.

"Such a tiny waist – she might snap in two!" whispered the other spitefully, and they both roared with laughter.

When the banquet was served the prince insisted that Cinderella sit next to him, and after dinner they danced again. Cinderella was enjoying herself so much she forgot all about the time. It was only when the clock struck midnight that she remembered her godmother's warning. She fled from the ballroom without a backward glance. The prince hurried after her but she ran faster than he. As she sped down the steps her ballgown turned to rags and she dropped one of her glass slippers. The prince picked it up. By the time she reached home, Cinderella was exhausted.

Soon her sisters arrived home. "There was the most beautiful princess at the ball," said one.

"The prince fell in love with her, and he was deeply saddened when she left at midnight," said the other.

As for the prince, he spent all night with the glass slipper pressed to his cheek, mourning the loss of the most wonderful girl he had ever set eyes upon. The next morning he was determined to find her. He sent his servant to all corners of the kingdom. "I will marry the girl whose foot fits the slipper," he declared. Well, every princess, duchess and lady in the land tried on the slipper, but none of them could fit the tiny shoe on her foot.

At last the servant called at the house of Cinderella and her stepsisters. "Me first!" they cried, pushing each other out of the way. One sister tried on the slipper but her toes were so fat that she couldn't squeeze them into the dainty shoe. Then the other sister tried, but her toes were so long they wouldn't fit either.

Cinderella had been watching from her corner by the fire. Now she came forward. "May I try on the shoe?" she asked timidly.

The stepsisters shrieked, "Don't be absurd! You weren't even at the ball."

But the prince's servant said, "If you wish to try on the slipper, then you shall." Cinderella slid her foot into the glass slipper and of course it fitted perfectly. The stepsisters were completely speechless with rage.

At that moment there was a flash of bright light and Cinderella's fairy godmother appeared. She touched Cinderella with her magic wand and immediately the girl's rags were transformed into the ballgown that she had worn the night before. Then her sisters recognised the beautiful princess they had seen at the ball. They fell upon their knees and begged forgiveness for the way they had treated her, hoping that they, too, might be invited to the palace. The servant escorted Cinderella to the palace and when the prince saw her, he immediately asked her to marry him. At the wedding there was much rejoicing and the sisters were so well behaved that they, too, received marriage proposals and they all lived happily ever after.

The Toys That Ran Away

"Put your toys away, Lucy," said Lucy's mother from the kitchen, "it's time to get ready for bed."

Lucy gave a great big sigh. "Do I really have to?" she asked, knowing full well what the answer was going to be.

"Yes, of course you do," said her mother. "You shouldn't have to be told each time to put your toys away. You really don't look after them properly."

It was true. Lucy never had been very good at looking after her toys. Once she left her beautiful new doll outside in her pram and she had become ruined after it rained. Then she had carelessly dropped her tea set on the floor and some of the cups had broken. And she was forever just pushing all her toys back

in the cupboard in a hurry, instead of putting them away carefully. Worse still, when she was in a temper, she would throw her toys, and sometimes she would even kick them.

Tonight Lucy was in another of her 'can't be bothered' moods. She grabbed a handful of toys and threw them into the cupboard. In first went some dolls, which all landed on their heads and then fell in a heap. Next Lucy threw in the little tables and chairs from the doll's house. They landed with a bounce and came to a stop in the corner. Without even looking behind her, Lucy then picked up some puzzles and a skipping rope, and tossed them into the cupboard, too. They landed with a crash on the floor of the cupboard as well.

"That's that," said Lucy. She closed the cupboard door, squashing the toys even more, and went into the bathroom to have her bath.

Inside the toy cupboard Teddy, one of the toys, spoke. "I'm not going to stay here a moment longer," he said.

"Nor me," said Katie the ragdoll.

107

"If we aren't going to be loved, we aren't staying either," chimed the doll's house furniture.

"I want to be somewhere where I'm not thrown around," said one of the puzzles.

"So do we," said the roller blades.

One after another, all the toys agreed that they weren't going to stay. They decided they would all go back to Toyland and wait to be given to some children who would love them more.

The next morning, Lucy decided that she would play with her skipping rope. When she opened the toy cupboard, she couldn't believe her eyes. All the toys had vanished. The shelves were completely empty.

At first Lucy thought her mother had moved them, but her mother said she hadn't. "I expect you've put them somewhere yourself, Lucy, and can't remember where you've left them," said her mother, not very helpfully. All day, Lucy searched high and low for her missing toys, but they were nowhere to be found. She went to bed in tears that night, wondering if she would ever be able to play with her toys again. She was already missing them terribly.

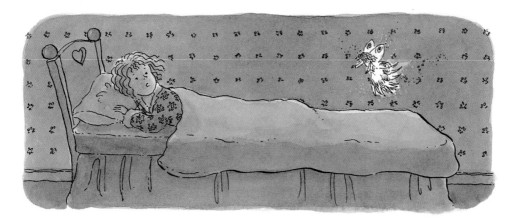

That night, Lucy was suddenly woken by a noise in her bedroom. Was she seeing things or was that a little fairy at the bottom of her bed? "Who are you?" asked Lucy.

"I am the special messenger from Toyland," replied the fairy. "I have been sent to tell you that all your toys have run away back to Toyland, because you treated them badly."

"Oh, I do miss my toys so much," cried Lucy.

"Well, if you really do, then you had better come and tell them yourself," said the fairy.

With that, the fairy floated over to Lucy and took her hand. The fairy then beat her wings so fast that they became a blur. At the same time Lucy felt herself being lifted from her bed. Out of Lucy's bedroom window they both flew, across fields and forests, until it became too misty for Lucy to see anything at all.

Suddenly, they were floating down to the ground. The mist lifted, and Lucy found herself in the grounds of a huge fairy-tale castle with tall, pointed turrets and warm, yellow lights twinkling from the windows.

"This is Toyland Castle," exclaimed the fairy, as she led Lucy to a large red door.

The fairy knocked on the door. "Do enter, please," said a voice.

Lucy found herself in a large, cosy room with a huge log fire. Sitting in the corner was a kindly looking little man wearing a carpenter's apron and holding a broken wooden doll. "Hello," he said, "you've come to ask your toys to return, haven't you?"

"Well... er... yes," said Lucy, not really quite knowing what to say.

"It's up to them to decide, of course," said the little man. "They only come back here if they are mistreated. If they are broken, I repair them, and then they go to other children who love them more."

"But I *do* love my toys," wept Lucy.

"Then come and tell them yourself," smiled the little man.

He led Lucy into another room, and there, to her surprise, were all her toys. Not only that, but they were all shiny and new again. Nothing was broken or chipped or scratched.

Lucy ran up to her toys. "Please, toys, please come home again. I really do love you and miss you, and I promise I shall never mistreat you again," she cried. She picked up Teddy and gave him a big hug. Then she did the same thing to all the other toys.

"Well, it's up to the toys now," said the little man. "You must go back home again with the fairy messenger and hope that they will give you another chance."

With that, the fairy messenger took Lucy's hand, and soon they were floating over her own garden again and through her bedroom window. Lucy was so tired she didn't even remember falling asleep when she got into bed.

In the morning she awoke, still rather sleepy, and rushed to the toy cupboard. There, neatly lined up on the shelves, were all her toys. Lucy was overjoyed. From that day on, she always treated her toys well and took great care of them.

Lucy never was quite sure whether the whole thing was a dream or not, but it certainly did the trick whatever it was. There was one thing that really puzzled her though. If it had just been a dream, why were all the toys so shiny and new again?

The Castle in the Clouds

There was once a family that lived in a little house in a village at the bottom of a mountain. At the top of the mountain was a great, grey castle made of granite. The castle was always shrouded in clouds, so it was known as the castle in the clouds. From the village you could only just see the outline of its high walls and turrets. No-one in the village ever went near the castle, for it looked such a gloomy and forbidding place.

Now in this family there were seven children. One by one they went out into the world to seek their fortune, and at last it was the youngest child's turn. His name was Sam. His only possession was a pet cat named Jess, and she was an excellent rat-catcher. Sam was most upset at the thought of leaving Jess behind when he went off to find work, but then he had an idea.

"I'll offer Jess's services at the castle in the clouds. They're bound to need a good ratter, and I'm sure I can find work there, too," he thought.

His parents were dismayed to discover that Sam intended to seek work at the castle, but try as they might they could not change his mind. So Sam set off for the castle with Jess at his side. Soon the road started to wind up the mountainside through thick pine forests. It grew cold and misty. Rounding a bend they suddenly found themselves up against a massive, grey stone wall. They followed the curve of the wall until they came to the castle door.

Sam went up to the door and banged on it. The sound echoed spookily. "Who goes there?" said a voice.

Looking up, Sam saw that a window high in the wall had been thrown open and a face was eyeing him suspiciously.

113

"I… I… I wondered if you'd be interested in employing my cat as a rat-catcher," began Sam.

The window slammed shut, but a moment later a hand beckoned him through the partly open castle door. Stepping inside, Sam and Jess found themselves face-to-face with an old man. "Rat-catcher, did you say?" said the old man raising one eyebrow. "Very well, but she'd better do a good job or my master will punish us all!"

Sam sent Jess off to prove her worth. In the meantime Sam asked the old man, who was the castle guard, if there might be any work for him, too.

"You can help out in the kitchens. It's hard work, mind!" the guard said.

Sam was soon at work in the kitchens – and what hard work it was! He spent all day peeling vegetables, cleaning pans and scrubbing the floor. By midnight he was exhausted. He was about to find a patch of straw to make his bed, when he noticed Jess wasn't around. He set off in search of her. Down dark passages he went, up winding staircases, looking in every corner and behind every door, but there was no sign of her. By now he was hopelessly lost and was wondering how he would ever find his way back to the kitchens, when he caught sight of Jess's green eyes shining like lanterns at the top of a rickety spiral staircase. "Here, Jess!" called Sam softly. But Jess stayed just where she was.

When he reached her, he found that she was sitting outside a door and seemed to be listening to something on the other side. Sam put his ear to the door. He could hear the sound of sobbing. He knocked gently at the door. "Who is it?" said a girl's voice.

"I'm Sam, the kitchen boy. What's the matter? Can I come in?" said Sam.

"If only you could," sobbed the voice. "I'm Princess Rose. When my father died my uncle locked me in here so that he could steal the castle. Now I fear I shall never escape!"

Sam pushed and pushed at the door, but to no avail. "Don't worry," he said, "I'll get you out of here."

Sam knew exactly what to do, for when he had been talking to the guard, he had spotted a pair of keys hanging on a nail in the rafters high above the old man's head. He had wondered at the time why anyone should put keys out of the reach of any human hand. Now he thought he knew – but first he had to get the keys himself!

Sam and Jess finally made their way back to where the keys were, only to find the guard was fast asleep in his chair right underneath them! Quick as a flash, Jess had leaped up on to the shelf behind his head. From there, she climbed higher and higher until she reached the rafters. She took the keys in her jaws and carried them gingerly down. But as she jumped from the shelf again, she knocked over a jug and sent it crashing to the floor. The guard woke with a start. "Who goes there?" he growled. He just caught sight of the tip of Jess's tail as she made a dash for the door.

Sam and Jess retraced their steps with the guard in hot pursuit. "You go a different way," hissed Sam, running up the stairs to Rose's door, while the old man disappeared off after Jess. Sam put one of the keys in the lock. It fitted! He turned the key and opened the door. There stood the loveliest girl he had ever seen. The princess ran towards him, as he cried, "Quick!

116

There's not a moment to lose." He grabbed her hand and led her out of the tower.

"Give me the keys," she said. She led him down to the castle cellars. At last they came to a tiny door. The princess put the second key in the lock and the door opened. Inside was a small cupboard, and inside that was a golden casket filled with precious jewels. "My own casket – stolen by my uncle," cried Rose.

Grabbing the casket the pair ran to the stables and saddled a horse. Suddenly Jess appeared with the guard still chasing him. With a mighty leap Jess landed on the back of the horse behind the princess and Sam. "Off we go!" cried Sam.

And that was the last that any of them saw of the castle in the clouds. Sam married the princess and they all lived happily ever after.

Rusty's Big Day

Long ago there lived a poor farmer called Fred, who had a horse called Rusty. Once Rusty had been a good, strong horse. He had willingly pulled the plough and taken his master into town to sell his vegetables. Now he was too old to work on the farm, but the farmer couldn't bear to think of getting rid of him because he was so sweet-natured. "It would be like turning away one of my own family," Fred used to say. Rusty spent his days grazing in the corner of the field. He was quite content, but he felt sad that he was no longer able to help the poor farmer earn his living.

One day, Fred decided to go to town to sell a few vegetables. He harnessed Beauty, the young mare, to the wagon and off they went. Beauty shook her fine mane and tossed a glance at Rusty as if to say, "Look who's queen of the farmyard!"

While Fred was in the town, his eye was caught by a notice pinned to a tree. It said:

Horse Parade at 2 pm today
The winner will pull the king's carriage
to the Grand Banquet tonight

"There's not a moment to lose, my girl!" said Fred. "We must get you ready for the parade." So saying, he turned the wagon around. "Giddy-up, Beauty!" he called, and she trotted all the way back to the farm.

Fred set to work to make Beauty look more lovely than she had ever done before. He scrubbed her hoofs and brushed her coat until it shone. Then he plaited her mane and tied it with a bright red ribbon. Rusty watched from the field. "How fine she looks," he thought, wistfully. "She's sure to win." He felt a bit sad that he was too old to take part in the parade, so he found a patch of the sweetest grass to graze on, to console himself.

All at once, he heard Fred approach. "Come on, old boy," he said, "you can come, too. It'll be fun for you to watch the parade, won't it?" Rusty was thrilled. It seemed such a long time since the master  had last taken him into town. Fred brushed Rusty's coat, too. "You want to look your best, don't you now, old boy?" he said. Soon the three of them set off back into town, with Fred riding on Beauty's back and Rusty walking by their side. When they reached the parade ground, there were already a lot of horses gathered there with their owners. There were horses of every shape and size – small, skinny ones, big, muscular ones and there were even big, skinny ones, too!

Soon it was time for the parade to begin. The king entered the parade ground, followed by the members of the royal court. They took their places at one end of the ground. Then the king announced three contests. First there would be a race. The horses would gallop from one end of the parade ground to the other.

Then there would be a contest of strength. Each horse would have to try and pull a heavy carriage. Lastly, there would be a trotting competition. Each horse would have to carry a rider around the parade ground.

The competition began. All the horses lined up at the starting line. "Come on, Rusty. Have a go!" whispered Fred. He led Rusty and Beauty to where the other horses were lined up.

All the other horses turned and stared. "What's an old horse like you doing taking part in a contest like this?" one of them asked disdainfully.

"You won't make it past the starting line!" taunted another.

Rusty said nothing and took his place at the start. Then they were off down the field. Rusty felt his heart pounding and his feet fly like never before, but try as he might he just couldn't keep up with the others and came in last.

"What did you expect?" snorted the other horses turning their backs on poor old Rusty.

However, Rusty was not downcast. "Speed isn't everything," he said to himself.

Now it was time for the test of strength. One by one the horses took it in turns to pull the carriage. When it was Rusty's turn, he tried his best. He felt every muscle in his aching body strain, as he slowly pulled the carriage along.

"Not a hope!" declared the other horses.

"Strength isn't everything," said Rusty to himself.

Next it was time for the trotting competition. "I shall ride each horse in turn," declared the king. He climbed up on to the first horse, but it bolted away so fast that the king was left hanging by the stirrups. The next horse lifted his legs so high that he threw the king right up in the air and he might have hurt himself badly, if he hadn't been caught by one of his courtiers. The next horse was so nervous about carrying the king that his teeth chattered, and the king had to put his fingers in his ears. Then it was Beauty's turn and she carried the king magnificently, until she stumbled at the end. At last it was Rusty's turn. The other horses sniggered, "Let's see that old horse make a fool of himself!"

Rusty carried the king quite slowly and steadily, making sure he picked his feet up carefully, so that his royal highness would not be jolted. "Thank you for a most pleasant ride," said the king dismounting. There was a hush as the horses and their owners awaited the result of the contest. "I have decided," announced the king, "that Rusty is the winner. Not only did he give me a most comfortable ride, but he accepted his other defeats with dignity. Speed and strength are not everything, you know."

Rusty and Fred were overjoyed, and even Beauty offered her congratulations. "Though I might have won if I hadn't stumbled," she muttered.

So Rusty proudly pulled the king's carriage that evening, and he made such a good job of it that the king asked him if he would do it again the following year. Then the king asked Fred if his daughter could ride Beauty from time to time. He even gave Fred a bag of gold to pay for the horses' upkeep. So the three of them were happy as they never had been before as they returned home to the farm that night.

Morag the Witch

Morag was just an ordinary witch – until the day she enrolled for a course of advanced spell casting at the Wizard, Witch and Warlock Institute of Magic. For that was where she met Professor Fizzlestick. Now Professor Fizzlestick was a very wise old man indeed. Morag, on the other hand, was a very vain young witch who didn't know as much as she thought she did. She could turn people into frogs if they really deserved it, and do other simple spells like that, but she still had a lot to learn. The problem was, Morag thought she was the most perfect little witch in the whole wide world.

Morag's adventure started on her very first day at school. At the beginning of the day, after all the young witches and wizards had made friends and met the teachers, they were called in one by one to talk to Professor Fizzlestick.

"Now, young Morag Bendlebaum, I taught both your mother and your father," said the professor in a very serious voice, "and a very fine witch and wizard they turned out to be, too. So, what kind of witch do you think you are going to be?"

Without giving this any thought at all, Morag blurted out, "I'm better than my parents, and I'm probably better than you!"

This answer surprised even Morag, for although she thought this was true, she didn't actually mean to say it.

"Don't be surprised by your answers," said Professor Fizzlestick, "there is a truth spell in this room, and whatever you truly believe you must say. And I have to say that you appear to have an enormously high opinion of yourself. Why don't you tell me what makes you so very good?"

"I'm clever," said Morag, "and I'm good, and I'm always right."

"But what about your dark side?" said Professor Fizzlestick.

"I'm sorry to disappoint you," replied Morag quite seriously, "but I'm afraid I simply don't have a dark side."

125

"Well in that case I would like you to meet someone very close to you," said Professor Fizzlestick with a smile on his lips.

Morag looked over to where Professor Fizzlestick pointed, and was startled to see on the sofa next to her... herself!

As Morag stared open-mouthed with astonishment, the professor explained that if, as she believed, she was without a dark side, then there was absolutely nothing to worry about. "If, however," he continued, "you have deceived yourself, then I'm afraid you are in for a few surprises."

With that the professor dismissed them both from the room and told them to get to know each other. As Morag and her dark side stood outside the professor's room, Morag's dark side jumped and whooped for joy. "At last," she cried, "I'm free. I don't have to sit and listen to you telling me what's right all day; I don't have to keep persuading you to choose the biggest slice of cake before your brother – in fact, I don't, I repeat **don't,** have to do anything that you tell me at all."

So saying she broke into a run and rushed down the corridor, knocking over chairs and bumping into other little witches and wizards along the way. Morag was horrified. She would have to follow her dark side and stop her from causing trouble. Morag chased after her dark side and finally caught up with her at the chocolate machine. "Don't eat all that chocolate," cried Morag. "You know it's bad for your teeth and will ruin your appetite for lunch!"

"Tsk!" scoffed her dark side. "You might not want any chocolate but I certainly do!" And with that she ran off once more, dropping chocolate on to the freshly polished floor as well as pushing a big piece into her mouth.

Just then, the bell sounded for lunch. Although Morag felt she ought to find her dark side, she also knew that the bell was a command to go to the dining hall, and she mustn't disobey it. Morag sat down to lunch next to her friend, Topaz. She was just about to tell her what had happened, when she saw that Topaz was not eating her vegetables! Morag scolded Topaz for this, and gave her a lecture on eating healthily.

Topaz stared at Morag in amazement, then peered closely at her. "What's happened to you?" she asked.

Morag explained what had happened in Professor Fizzlestick's office, and then declared, "And you know, it's the best thing that has ever happened to me. I thought I was good before, but now I'm even better. I never want my dark side back again, but we must find her and lock her up so that she can do no harm."

Topaz agreed that they must find her dark side, but secretly hoped that she and Morag would be re-united. Morag wasn't Morag without her dark side.

After lunch, Morag went for her first lesson of the afternoon. When she walked into the classroom she discovered her dark side already there, busy preparing spells! Morag's dark side had already prepared a 'turning a nose into an elephant's trunk' spell and a 'turning skin into dragons' scales' spell and was just finishing off a 'turning your teacher into stone' spell!

Morag suddenly heard a trumpeting noise from the back of the classroom. She turned to find that the wizard twins, Denzil and Dorian Dillydally, had both sprouted huge grey trunks down to the ground where their noses had been. Morag rushed over to her dark side to make her change them back, but before she could reach her she tripped over a creature crouching down on the floor. It looked just like a dragon and it was wearing a purple and white spotted dress last seen on Betina Bumblebag. Morag's dark side was casting spells all over the place. "Oh, why doesn't the teacher stop her!" cried Morag to Topaz.

I'm sure you've guessed by now. Nice Miss Chuckle was entirely turned to stone from head to foot!

Just then Professor Fizzlestick walked into the classroom. Morag pointed to her dark side, still making spells at the front of the classroom.

"Lock her up immediately," Morag begged the professor.

"I'm afraid that you are the only one who can do that," said the wise old man. "The two of you are inseparable and you need each other. Without your dark side you would be unbearable and without you she is dreadful. Have I your permission to lock her back inside you?"

Even though Morag didn't want any part of her dark side back, she agreed reluctantly. Her dark side instantly disappeared, and Morag felt... wonderful! Oh, it was so good to be back to normal, to be basically good, but occasionally mischievous.

"Thank you," said Morag to the professor. "I think I've learned something very valuable today."

"There is good and bad in everyone," replied the professor, "even the most perfect of witches."

Morag blushed when she remembered what she had said earlier that morning, but she was so relieved to find she was normal that she really didn't mind. Morag and Topaz went back to the classroom to undo all the bad things Morag's dark side had done, but on the way they both felt a huge urge for a snack, so they stopped at the chocolate machine first!

The Dog With No Voice

There once lived a prince whose words were pure poetry. He amused the court with his witty, rhyming verse, yet his kind and thoughtful words made him popular with all. It was said he could even charm the birds from the trees.

One day, he was walking in the forest when he came upon an old lady with a huge bundle on her back. "Let me help," said the prince. He took the load and walked along beside the woman. They chatted away and before long they had reached the old lady's door.

Now the old lady – who was really a witch – had been listening intently to the prince's words. "What a fine voice he has!" she thought to herself. "I would like my own son to speak like that. Then maybe he could find himself a wealthy wife and we'd be rich for ever more!"

"You must be thirsty," she said to the prince. "Let me give you something to quench your thirst to repay you for your kindness." The prince gratefully accepted, and was given a delicious drink which he drained to the last drop. He was about to thank the witch when he began to feel very peculiar. He found he was getting smaller and smaller. He looked down at his feet and saw two hairy paws. Then he turned round and saw to his horror that he had grown a shaggy tail! He tried to shout at the witch but all that came out of his mouth was a loud bark!

The witch hugged herself for joy. "My spell worked!" she cackled. "Come here my son!" she called.

There appeared at the door a rough-looking young man. "What's going on, my dearest mother?" he said in a voice that sounded familiar to the prince. Then he looked down and exclaimed, "Where did you find this poor little dog?"

Now the prince understood what had happened. "The old lady has turned me into a humble hound and given my voice to her son. Whatever am I to do?" he thought miserably. "I can't return to the palace. They'll never let a stray dog in." He turned with his tail between his legs and trotted off forlornly into the forest.

The witch and her son were delighted with his new voice. She made him scrub himself clean from top to toe and dressed him in the prince's clothes. "Now go," she said, "and don't return until you've found a rich girl to marry!"

The young man set off, eager to try out his new voice. Soon he was feeling very pleased with himself as he talked to passers-by. "What a very polite young man!" and "What a wonderful way with words," folk cried. "He could charm the birds out of the trees," other people said.

The witch's son travelled far and wide until at last he came to a castle where he spied a fair princess sitting on her balcony. He called to her and straight away she arose and looked down into the garden, enraptured by the sound of his beautiful voice. She was enchanted by his fine words and guessed they must belong to a prince. Soon the princess and the witch's son were chatting away merrily, and to his delight when he asked her to marry him she readily agreed. "For one with so beautiful a voice," she thought to herself, "must indeed be a fine young man."

Meanwhile, the poor dog-prince wandered in the forest, surviving as best he could by foraging for roots and fruits in the undergrowth. Feeling truly miserable, he stopped to drink from a stream. As he dipped his long dog's tongue in the cool water, he caught sight of someone sitting on a bridge. It was a pixie, fishing with a tiny net.

"Cheer up!" said the little fellow, "I saw everything that happened and I think I know how we can get your voice back. Follow me!" And with that he was off, dancing away through the forest with the dog-prince trotting along behind. They seemed to go on forever, and the dog-prince was feeling very hot, and the pads of his paws were quite sore, by the time they reached the castle. He could see the witch's son in the garden calling to the princess on the balcony. The dog-prince's eyes filled with tears, for she was quite the loveliest girl he had ever seen and he wished he could marry her himself.

"We will be married today," the witch's son was saying in the prince's voice, "I will await you by the church, my fairest one." Seizing his fishing net, the pixie leaped high in the air. As the words 'my fairest one' floated up to the balcony, he caught them in the net and gave them back to the dog-prince.

As soon as he had swallowed the words, the dog-prince could speak again. "Thank you, little pixie," he cried, "but what can I do? Now I am a dog with a prince's voice. The princess will never marry me."

"If you want to break the witch's spell, you must go to the church – fast!" said the pixie. And with those words he disappeared.

Straight away, the dog-prince ran to the church door. There was the princess looking most perplexed, for standing beside her was the witch's son – with not a word in his head. "I don't understand," she cried, "I thought I was to marry a silver–tongued young man, but now I find he is a dumb ragamuffin!"

"I can explain," exclaimed the dog-prince.

The princess spun around. "Who can explain?" she asked, for all she could see was a dog in front of her. "What a handsome dog!" she cried, bending down and kissing him on the nose. To her astonishment, the dog's hairy paws and shaggy tail immediately disappeared and there stood the prince. "But you're... but he..." she stammered looking from the prince to the witch's son.

Well, the prince explained everything that had happened, and after that he and the princess were married with great rejoicing. And as for the witch's son? He wasn't a bad young man, really, so the prince taught him to speak again – with a beautiful voice – and he married the princess's younger sister.

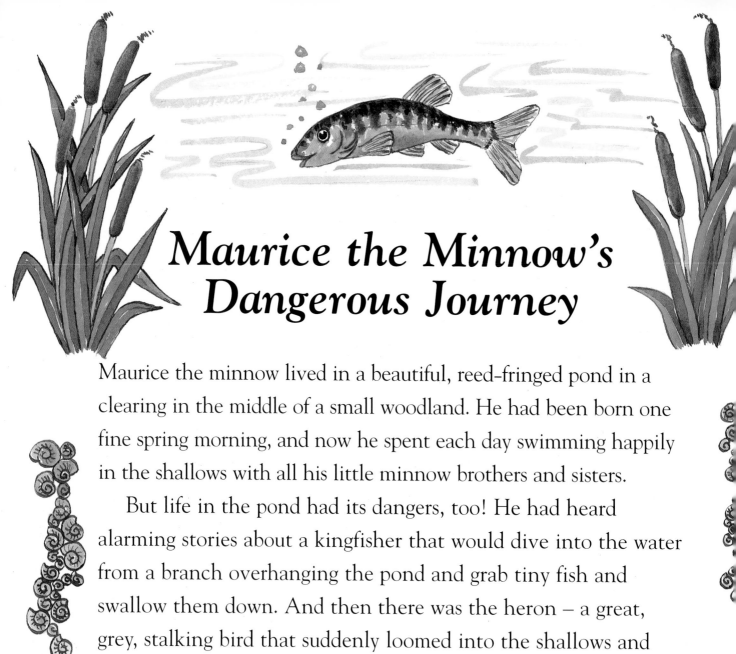

Maurice the Minnow's Dangerous Journey

Maurice the minnow lived in a beautiful, reed-fringed pond in a clearing in the middle of a small woodland. He had been born one fine spring morning, and now he spent each day swimming happily in the shallows with all his little minnow brothers and sisters.

But life in the pond had its dangers, too! He had heard alarming stories about a kingfisher that would dive into the water from a branch overhanging the pond and grab tiny fish and swallow them down. And then there was the heron – a great, grey, stalking bird that suddenly loomed into the shallows and snatched unsuspecting fish with its great beak.

But the stories Maurice feared most were the ones about Lucius the pike. Lucius had lived in the pond for longer than anyone could remember. Woe betide you if you met Lucius when he was hungry, for he would dart out from his hiding place among the water weeds, and you would be gone! Nothing ever escaped from his huge jaws, which were lined with needle-sharp teeth. Maurice had heard tales of Lucius swallowing fish bigger than Maurice could imagine – not to mention ducks, voles and other animals of the pond. Why, there was even a rumour that Lucius had once snatched a dog from the bank and taken it down to the depths of the pond to devour it!

Maurice's mother had said that the best way to avoid meeting Lucius was to always stay in the shallows, and never swim across the pond, for it was in the deep, dark waters that Lucius loved to hunt.

One sunny summer's day, Maurice and his brothers and sisters were swimming in the shallows as usual, when suddenly he felt himself being lifted up and out of the water. The next thing he knew he was flapping helplessly in the bottom of a net, gasping for breath. Mercifully, he soon found himself back in the water again, but it seemed different now. It was light all around and there were no welcoming, sheltering weeds to hide in. And where were all his brothers and sisters? Next, to his horror, he saw a huge, unfamiliar creature staring at him. He'd heard no stories about anything as big as this! The creature's head seemed so close that Maurice felt certain he was about to be eaten. But just as suddenly the creature seemed to move away, and Maurice felt himself being carried along in this new, strange, watery world.

Maurice was wondering if he was to be trapped in this new, small pond forever when just as suddenly as he seemed to have

entered the pond, he was now leaving it again. He felt himself falling down, down, until – with a splash – he was back in his own pond again. Or at least, it seemed like his pond, but nothing was quite as familiar as it had been. Finding a clump of water weed, he immediately dived under it for safety, while he considered what to do next.

"Hello, you're new here, aren't you?" a friendly voice said. Maurice looked round in surprise to find himself face to face with a frog. He told the frog about his horrible adventure while the frog listened patiently, nodding wisely from time to time.

"Well, we know what's happened to you, don't we?" said the frog when Maurice had finished. "You got caught in a little boy's fishing net. They're often about around here. I've no doubt the big creature you saw was just the little boy looking at you swimming in his jam jar full of water. And now he's decided to put you back. The only trouble is, you're far from home. You live on the other side of the pond. And to get you back means we have got to go on a very dangerous journey."

139

Maurice didn't like the sound of this at all, but he missed his family terribly and knew that he would never be able to get back home without the kind frog's help. So without more ado, the two of them set off for their journey across the deep, dark pond.

"Swim near the surface. It's safer," advised the frog, "but keep a close eye out for kingfishers."

They seemed to have been swimming for ages, when suddenly a great, dark shadow appeared beneath them.

"It's Lucius!" cried the frog in fright.

Before either of them could escape, they found themselves face to face with the dreaded pike. "Well, well," leered Lucius. "I can't believe my luck! A frog *and* a minnow. Lunch and supper together if I'm not mistaken!"

So saying, he opened his enormous jaws and was about to swallow them whole when – BOINK! – a huge, flat stone landed right on Lucius's head. Dazed, Lucius sank slowly towards the bottom of the pond.

"Quick! It's our chance to escape!" yelled the frog. The two friends swam for their lives. Maurice kept thinking that any moment Lucius would reappear, but he needn't have worried. Lucius had too big a headache to think about hunting for a while yet!

Then suddenly Maurice was home. He recognised his own little part of the pond, and there swimming in the shallows was his family.

"I can't thank you enough," said Maurice gratefully to the frog. "But what *did* happen to Lucius?"

"You can thank the little boy who caught you in the net for our escape," said the frog. "He was skimming stones across the pond and luckily Lucius's head got in the way!"

Maurice decided that he'd had quite enough adventures for one day, and found himself a cosy piece of water weed to hide under. Soon he was fast asleep.

The Mirror of Dreams

The house on the corner of Nightingale Avenue was tall and very handsome, and was by far the largest in the neighbourhood. From the street you could see four floors of beautifully decorated rooms, and if you peeped over the railings you could see the basement below. If you were lucky enough to be asked into the house, and passed through the beautiful hallways into the playroom, you might meet the owner's daughter, Cordelia. Sometimes Cordelia would be sitting in her silk pyjamas playing on her grand piano, and sometimes she would be dressed in the finest velvet gowns playing with her lovely dolls.

If you went down the stairs and into the basement, you might come across Polly. Polly's mother was a chambermaid in the house, and worked hard all day long to make the house sparkling clean. Sometimes Polly helped her to polish the ornaments and dust the furniture, but more often Polly sat on her own in her small bedroom drawing pictures with some crayons on a drawing pad she had been given for her birthday. When Polly was helping to polish the furniture she would look longingly at all of

Cordelia's fine clothes and toys, and when she sat alone in her room she would draw pictures of all the beautiful things she would like to own if only she could afford them.

One day, a large parcel was delivered to the house and taken upstairs to Cordelia's bedroom. A little while later, Cordelia's maid carried a pretty, ornate mirror down from her room and put it with the rubbish waiting for collection outside the house. Polly asked the maid why the mirror was to be thrown away, and the maid explained that Cordelia had been given a new mirror in which to brush her long, silky locks, and that she didn't need it any more. The maid then asked if Polly would like the old mirror, and of course Polly accepted with pleasure – it was the most beautiful thing she had ever owned.

Polly carried the mirror back to her room and polished it lovingly. As she polished the glass a strange thing started to happen. The glass went misty, and then cleared as her own reflection stared back at her once more. But the reflection that stared back was not dressed in rags and worn old clothes as Polly was, but in a rich gown of the most beautiful cream satin, with pink bows and apricot lace.

Polly was entranced. She looked almost as beautiful as Cordelia! Her hair gleamed and her fingers were white and magnificent. As she looked further into the mirror, she saw herself dancing at a ball, and then sitting down to eat the finest food she had ever seen – hams and roasted meats, and cakes of strawberries and cream!

And then the mirror spoke to her. "I am the Mirror of Dreams," the cool, clear voice said. "Whatever your heart desires most will be reflected in my shiny surface."

Polly was astounded, but so happy. She didn't care that it was only a day dream, for when she saw her reflection in the beautiful clothes, she felt as if she were truly there dancing and eating the fine foods – she could almost taste the fruit and cream in her mouth!

From that day on, Polly sat in her room every day, and dreamed and dreamed and dreamed. She had never felt so happy before, and could not wait to wake up each morning to visit her imaginary world. She certainly didn't understand how Cordelia

could have thrown away such a magical wonder, and thought that she could not have known of its enchanting secret. She supposed also that Cordelia could have had no use for such a mirror, for whatever Cordelia wanted in real life she received, and would have no need to dream. But Polly was to find out that this was very far from true!

Weeks passed, and every day Polly sat and dreamed of ermine cloaks, of diamonds and pearls, of parties and picnics and carnivals. Eventually, she had dreamed every dream she had ever wanted. And Polly began to realise that it no longer made her as happy as it once had, and she began to grow weary of her Mirror of Dreams. She sat in front of the mirror less and less, and eventually when she did visit the mirror she could not think of a single thing that would make her happy. Even the dreams she had in which her mother wore fine silk clothes and didn't have to scrub and clean for their living could no longer make her happy.

She preferred her real mother, who came to kiss her good night and read her stories no matter how tired and overworked she was. Eventually she stopped looking in the mirror altogether, and finally decided to throw the mirror away – it had only made her more unhappy.

As the long winter turned into spring she acted upon her decision, and took down the mirror to throw away with the rubbish. But as she looked into the glass, it misted over in its familiar way and she saw herself in the mirror as she looked in real life, but in it she was playing with other children like herself, and reading stories with them and sharing toys. She felt gloriously happy, and knew in that instant that all she wanted was a very good friend. She realised in that moment, too, that perhaps Cordelia really had known the mirror's secret, but that she also had become more unhappy as the dreams faded and reality forced itself upon her. She wondered aloud what it was that Cordelia had dreamed of, and for the second and last time the mirror spoke in its cool, clear voice.

"The Mirror of Dreams showed Cordelia her heart's desire, and her heart desires a true friend and companion – someone who is not jealous of her wealth, but a friend who will share her hopes and dreams, and with whom she can have parties, games and picnics."

Polly put the mirror down and thought with amazement that she could be that friend, if Cordelia would be friends with someone poor but honest and true. Polly left the mirror with the household rubbish and was about to make the descent back to the basement, when she saw Cordelia standing in the garden at the back of the house. Cordelia had seen her discard the mirror, and shyly walked up to Polly. Polly overcame her shyness also and went to meet Cordelia, and then she told her they shared the same dream.

Cordelia and Polly became the best of friends from that day on. They shared everything they had, no matter how much or little. They talked and laughed together all day long, and they played long into the evening. They didn't have to dream any more, for they had both got their true heart's desire.

147

Mr Mole Gets Lost

Mr Mole poked his little black nose out from the top of one of his mole hills and gave a great big sniff of the air. Then he sniffed again. And then a third time just to make sure. "Oh dear," he thought, "it smells like it's going to rain."

Mr Mole didn't like the rain one bit. Every time he got caught in the rain his plush little velvet fur coat got all wet and drippy, and he left muddy footprints all over his underground burrow. But worse still, the rain got in through the holes in his mole hills and then everything got all soggy and took days to dry out.

Well, the skies got darker and darker, and very soon little spots of rain began to fall. Then the spots became bigger. And then bigger still. Before long, all you could see before your eyes were big, straight rods of rain bouncing off the leaves on the trees, pounding the ground and turning everything muddy and wet.

Mr Mole had never seen rain like it. He sat in his burrow in the middle of the meadow wishing it would stop. But it just kept raining and raining. Soon the rain started entering his burrow. First it went drip, drip, drip through the holes in his mole hills, and then it became a little river of water in the bottom of his burrow. Then the little river became a bigger, faster-flowing river and suddenly Mr Mole was being washed along by it. Through the tunnels of his burrow he went, this way and then that, as the water gushed and poured through his underground home.

149

The next thing he knew he was being washed out of his burrow completely as the rain water carried him off down the meadow. Down he went, not knowing which way up he was or where he was going. Now he was being washed through the woods at the bottom of the meadow, but still the water carried him on, bouncing and turning him until he was dizzy and gasping for breath.

Suddenly, he came to a halt. The rain water gurgled and trickled around him and then flowed onwards, as he found himself stuck firmly in the branches of a bush. "Oh dear," Mr Mole said as he got himself free. "Goodness me, where can I be?" he thought. Mr Mole looked around him, but being a very short-sighted mole – as most moles are – he couldn't make out any of the places that were familiar to him. Worse still, he couldn't smell any smells that were familiar to him. He was completely lost, far from home, and had no idea how to get back again. Now, to make things worse, it was starting to get dark

"Woo-oo-oo-oo-oo!" said a voice suddenly. Mr Mole nearly jumped out of his moleskin with fright. "I wouldn't stay here if I were you," said the voice again. Mr Mole looked up and found himself face to face with an enormous owl. "Don't you know it's not safe in the woods at night?" asked the owl. "There are snakes and foxes and weasels and all sorts of nasty creatures that you really wouldn't like to meet."

"Oh dear!" was all Mr Mole could think of saying. He told the owl of his terrible watery journey and how he was lost and didn't know how to get back home again.

"You need to talk to Polly Pigeon," said the owl. "She is a homing pigeon and she lives near your meadow. She can show you the way home. But we'll have to find her first. Stay close to me, mind, and look out for those snakes, foxes and weasels I told you about."

Mr Mole didn't need telling twice. He stayed so close to the kindly owl that every time the owl stopped or turned round to talk to Mr Mole, Mr Mole bumped right into him!

Through the dark, dangerous woods they went. Every now and again, there would be an unfriendly noise, such as a deep growl or a hiss, coming from the dense, tangled trees, but Mr Mole didn't want to think about that too much, so he just made sure that he never lost sight of the owl.

Finally, just when Mr Mole thought that he couldn't go a step further, they came to a halt by an old elm tree.

"Hallo-oooo," called the owl.

They were in luck. Polly Pigeon was waking up, and they found her just in time for she was about to continue her journey home.

"Please," said Mr Mole, "I'm afraid I'm terribly lost and don't know how to get back to my meadow. Will you take me there?"

"Of course I will," said Polly Pigeon. "We'd better let you rest here a while first, though. But we must go before it gets light."

So Mr Mole was soon trudging wearily back to his meadow, following as closely behind Polly Pigeon as he was able. Just as the first rays of sun lit the morning sky, Mr Mole smelled a very familiar smell. It was his meadow! He was almost home!

Soon, he was back in his own burrow. It was so wet and muddy, however, that the first thing he did was build some new tunnels higher up the meadow so that the rain wouldn't wash down into them so easily. Then he settled down to eat one of his supplies of worms, and fell into a deep, well-earned slumber.

The Dragon Who Was Scared of Flying

Once upon a time, in a land far away, there lived a dragon named Dennis. He lived in a cave high up in the mountains. All his friends lived in caves nearby, and his own brothers and sisters lived right next door. Now you would think that Dennis would have been a very happy dragon, surrounded by his friends and family, wouldn't you? Well, I'm sorry to say that Dennis was, in fact, a very unhappy and lonely dragon.

The reason for this was that Dennis was scared of flying. Every day his friends would set off to have adventures, leaving poor Dennis behind on his own. Dennis would stare out of his cave at the departing dragons. How he wished he could join them!

After they had gone, he would stand on the ledge outside his cave, trying to build up the courage to fly. But as soon as he looked over the edge, he felt all giddy and had to step back. Then he would crawl back into his cave defeated and spend the rest of the day counting stalagtites on the ceiling or rearranging his collection of bat bones.

Every evening, the other dragons would return with amazing tales of what they had been up to that day. "I rescued a damsel in distress," one would say.

"I fought the wicked one-eyed giant and won," boasted another.

"I helped light the fire for a witch's cauldron," announced a third.

"What have you been up to?" Dennis's sister Doreen used to ask him.

155

"Oh... um... this and that," Dennis would reply mournfully, looking down at his scaly toes. Then Doreen would lead him out of the cave and try to teach him to fly. Dennis would take a running jump and flap his wings furiously but his feet would stay firmly on the ground. Then the other dragons would laugh so much that, in the end, he always gave up.

One day, Dennis could stand it no longer. The other dragons flew off as usual to find adventure but Dennis, instead of retreating into his cave, set off down the mountain side. It was very tiring having to walk. Dennis had never really been further than from his cave to the ledge and back, and soon he was puffing and panting. He was about to rest at the side of the path when his eye was caught by something colourful in the distance. Down in the valley he could make out some brightly coloured tents, and now he could hear the faint strains of music drifting up to him. "I'd better take a closer look," thought Dennis. "Maybe I can have an adventure, like the other dragons!" He got so excited at the thought of his very own adventure that he started to run. Then he got all out of breath and had to stop altogether for a while.

At last Dennis reached the tents and found himself in a world more exotic than he could ever have imagined. He was surrounded by strange, four-legged creatures, such as he had never seen before. There was a yellow creature that roared and another one with stripes and fierce teeth. There were also quite a few hairy creatures with long tails. These ones were dressed up to look like boys and girls. Can you guess what all these creatures were? Of course, Dennis had never seen a lion or a tiger or a chimpanzee before. He thought they were very peculiar! The animals thought Dennis was very odd, too. They stood in a circle around him. "How strange," snarled the lion. "A slimy thing with wings!"

"It doesn't look very fit!" growled the tiger, flexing his claws.

"Look at its funny, knobbly tail," giggled the chimpanzees.

Dennis began to feel unhappy and unwanted again, but at that moment he heard a friendly voice saying, "Hello, there! Welcome to Chippy's Circus. I'm Claude the clown. How do you do?"

Dennis turned round. Now he felt really confused, for standing behind him was a man with the unhappiest face Dennis had ever seen. He had great sad eyes and a mouth that was turned down so far that it seemed to touch his chin. Yet he spoke so cheerfully!

"I'm Dennis the dragon," said Dennis.

"A dragon, eh?" said Claude. "Well, we've never had a dragon in the circus before. Might be quite a crowd puller! Would you like to join the circus?" he asked.

"Oh, yes please," cried Dennis.

"Very well," said Claude. "I'm sure you're very talented," he added.

So Dennis joined the circus and was happy for the first time in his life. The other animals became quite friendly now that they knew what he was. Claude taught Dennis to ride the unicycle and to do acrobatic tricks. He also learned how to dive into a bucket of water. He didn't mind that a bit because his slimy skin was quite waterproof! Now, as you know, dragons are particularly good at breathing fire, so Dennis soon became the circus's champion fire-eater. Folk would come from far and near to see Dennis shooting flames high into the dark roof of the big top.

One evening Dennis had just finished his fire-eating act. He was eating an icecream to cool his hot throat and watching Carlotta, the tight-rope walker. She was pirouetting high up on the rope as usual. Then all at once she lost her footing and Dennis saw to his horror that she was going to fall. He dropped his icecream and, without thinking, flapped his wings furiously. As Carlotta fell, Dennis found himself flying up towards her. He caught her gently on his back and flew down to the ground with her clinging on tightly. The crowd roared and burst into applause. They obviously thought it was all part of the act.

"Thank you, Dennis," whispered Carlotta in Dennis's ear. "You saved my life."

Dennis was overjoyed. Not only had he saved Carlotta's life, he had also learned to fly. And he said with a grin, "I do declare that flying is actually rather fun."

159

The Very Big Parcel

Once upon a time there lived an old man and his wife. They dwelled in a small house with a small, neat garden and they were very contented. What's more, they had very good friends and neighbours, with whom they shared everything. One day, there was a knock at the door and there stood the postman with a huge parcel in his arms.

"My, oh my!" exclaimed the old man to his wife as he staggered into the kitchen with the enormous load.

"Whatever can it be?" wondered the old woman as the two of them stared at the parcel. "Perhaps it's a new set of china," said she.

"Or a new wheelbarrow," said he. And they began to think about all the fancy things there might be inside the parcel.

"Well, why don't we open it and see?" said the old lady at last. And so they did. They looked into the box and at first it seemed to be totally empty.

"Well, I never did!" cried the old man. And then he spotted something right in the corner of the box. He lifted it out into the light to examine it more carefully and discovered it was a single seed.

Well, the old man and his wife were most upset. Whereas before they were quite content, now that they had thought about all the things that might have been in the box they were bitterly disappointed by the seed. "Still," said the old man at last, "we'd better plant it anyway. Who knows, maybe we'll get a nice fresh lettuce from it."

So he planted the seed in the garden. Every day he watered the ground and soon a shoot appeared. The shoot grew into a strong young plant and then it grew taller and taller. Higher and higher it grew until it was a handsome tree. The man and his wife were excited to see fruits growing on the tree. "I wonder if they're apples," the old man said. Each day he watered the tree and examined the fruits. One day he said to his wife, "The first fruit is ready to pick." He carefully reached up into the tree and picked the large red fruit.

161

He carried it into the kitchen and put it on the table. Then he took a knife and cut the fruit in half. To his astonishment out poured a pile of gold coins. "Come quickly!" he called to his wife. Well, the pair of them danced round the kitchen for joy.

The old couple decided to spend just one gold coin and keep the rest. "After all," said the woman wisely, "we don't know what's in the other fruits. They may be full of worms." So they spent one golden penny in the town and put the rest aside.

The next day the old man picked another big red fruit and this, too, was full of gold. After that the old couple were less careful with their money, thinking all the fruits must be full of gold.

They had a wonderful time buying fine clothes and things for the house and garden. Each day the man picked another fruit. Each day it was full of gold and each day they went into town and had a grand time spending the money. But all the while the man forgot entirely to water the tree.

Meanwhile, the old couple's friends and neighbours started to gossip among themselves. They wondered where all the money was coming from and they began to resent the old couple. They noticed that the old couple didn't buy anything for their friends, or even throw a party. Gradually their friends ignored them until the old couple were left with no friends at all. But they didn't even notice because they were so busy spending the gold coins.

Then one day the old man looked out into the garden and saw that the tree was all withered. He rushed outside and threw bucket after bucket of water over the tree, but all to no avail.

He and his wife frantically picked the fruits left on the tree, but when they took them indoors they found to their dismay that they were cracked and gnarled. When they broke open the fruits they were full of dust. "If only I had not been so thoughtless and remembered to water the tree!" cried the old man in anguish.

The next day the old couple looked out of the window to find that the tree had vanished. Now what were they to do? They had completely neglected to take care of their garden and now they had nothing to eat. They realised that they would have to sell their riches to buy food. Then they also needed new gardening tools, for theirs had grown rusty with neglect.

As the weeks passed, the old man and his wife gradually sold all the fine things they had bought, just to keep body and soul together. They felt truly miserable and sorry for the way they had treated their neighbours. For now they realised just how lonely they were without their friends. "We have no money now," said the wife one day, "but let's have a party anyway. For friendship is more valuable than any amount of gold coins."

So the old couple invited all their friends and neighbours round and they had a grand party. The friends wondered what had happened to all the old couple's riches and what had happened to make the old couple so friendly once more, but I don't think they ever found out, do you?

 # The Golden Bird

There was once a king who kept a golden bird in a gilded cage. The bird wanted for nothing. Every day the king's servant brought him food and water and groomed his fine yellow feathers. And each day the bird sang his beautiful song for the king. "How lucky I am," cried the king, "to have such a beautiful bird that sings such a fine song." However, as time passed the king began to feel sorry for the bird. "It really isn't fair," he thought, "to keep such a handsome creature in a cage. I must give the bird its freedom." He called his servant and ordered him to take the cage into the jungle and release the bird.

The servant obeyed, and took the cage deep into the jungle where he came to a small clearing. He set the cage down, opened the door and out hopped the golden bird. "I hope you can look after yourself," the servant said as he walked away.

The golden bird looked about him. "This is strange!" he thought to himself. "Still, I suppose someone will come along to feed me soon." He settled down and waited.

After a while he heard a crashing sound in the trees, and then he saw a monkey swinging from branch to branch on his long arms.

"Hello there!" called the monkey, hanging by his tail and casting the bird an upside down grin. "Who are you?"

"I am the golden bird," replied the golden bird haughtily.

"I can see you're new around here," said the monkey. "I'll show you the best places to feed in the tree tops."

167

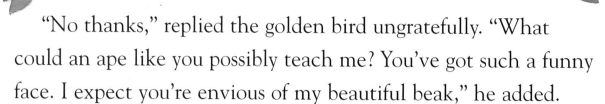

"No thanks," replied the golden bird ungratefully. "What could an ape like you possibly teach me? You've got such a funny face. I expect you're envious of my beautiful beak," he added.

"Have it your own way," called the monkey as he swung off into the trees.

Some time later the golden bird heard a hissing noise in the undergrowth and a snake came slithering by. "Well, hello," hissed the snake. "Who are you?"

"I am the golden bird," replied the golden bird proudly.

"Let me show you the jungle paths," said the snake.

"No thanks," replied the bird rudely. "What could a snake possibly teach me? With your horrid hissing voice, you must be jealous of my beautiful song," he said, forgetting that he had not opened his beak to sing yet.

"Very well," hissed the snake as he slithered away into the undergrowth.

By now the golden bird was beginning to wonder when his food would arrive. He began to imagine the tasty morsel that he hoped he would soon be eating. Just then he was aware of a movement on the tree trunk behind him. Looking up he caught a glimpse of a chameleon, lying camouflaged against the trunk.

"Good day," said the chameleon. "I've been here all the time, so I know who you are. You're the golden bird. I've heard you say it twice. It's a good idea to know where to hide in case of danger. Let me show you."

"No thanks," replied the golden bird. "What could an ugly brute like you possibly teach me? You must wish you had lovely feathers like me," he said, fluffing up his beautiful, golden plumage.

"Don't say I didn't warn you," muttered the chameleon as he darted away.

The golden bird had just settled down again when a great grey shadow passed over the jungle. He looked up to see an eagle swooping low over the trees. The monkey swung up to hide in the densest foliage near the top of the trees. The snake slid into the deepest part of the undergrowth. The chameleon stayed quite still but his skin colour became a perfect match for the tree he was on and he became totally invisible.

"Aha!" thought the golden bird. "All I have to do is fly away and that stupid eagle will never catch up with me." He flapped his wings and flapped and flapped, but he did not know that his wings had grown weak through living a life of luxury in the palace. Now the bird regretted his golden plumage and wished that he had dull brown feathers that would not show up in the forest clearing. For his fine yellow feathers made him easy to see. He was sure the eagle would come and gobble him up. "Help!" he trilled. "Please help me someone." Now he could see the eagle swooping down towards him with eyes blazing like fire and talons drawn.

170

At that moment the golden bird felt something close around his legs and pull him into the undergrowth. It was the snake. Then he was lifted up into the trees by a long, hairy arm and saw he was being carried by the monkey. "Keep still," whispered the chameleon pushing him into the centre of a large yellow flower. "The eagle won't see you there." And sure enough, the golden bird found that he was precisely the colour of the flower and the eagle flew straight past him.

"However can I repay you all?" exclaimed the bird. "You saved my life!"

"You can sing for us," replied the animals. And from then on, the monkey, the snake and the chameleon looked after the golden bird, and he sang his beautiful song for them every day.

Jimbo Comes Home

Jimbo the circus elephant was snoring away in his cage one night when he heard a strange noise. At first he thought it was part of his dream. In his dream he was walking across a hot, dusty plain while in the distance there was the sound of thunder.

All at once Jimbo was wide awake. He realised that he was in his cage after all and that what he thought was the sound of thunder was the noise of his cage on the move. Now this worried him, because the circus never moved at night. He rose to his feet and looked around. He could see men pulling on the tow bar at the front of the cage. These were strangers – it certainly wasn't Carlos his trainer! Jimbo started to bellow, "Help! Stop thief!" But it was too late. His cage was already rumbling out of the circus ground and down the road.

Eventually, the cage passed through a gate marked 'Zipper's Circus' and Jimbo knew what had happened. He had been stolen by the Zipper family, his own circus family's greatest rivals! Jimbo was furious. How had the thieves got away with it? Surely someone at Ronaldo's Circus must have heard them stealing him? But Jimbo waited in vain to be rescued.

The next morning, the thieves opened up Jimbo's cage and tried to coax him out, but he stayed put. In the end, after much struggling, they managed to pull him out. Once he was out of his cage, he took the biggest drink of water he could from a bucket and soaked his new keeper! He refused to cooperate, kicked over his food, and when he appeared in the circus that night he made sure he got all the tricks wrong.

"Don't worry," said Mr Zipper to Jimbo's new trainer, "he'll just take a little while to settle down. Soon he'll forget that he was once part of Ronaldo's Circus." But Jimbo didn't forget for, as you know, an elephant never forgets.

The other animals in Zipper's Circus had all been stolen from other circuses, too. "You'll just have to get used to it here," said one of the chimps to Jimbo. "It's not so bad really." But Jimbo decided he was going to try and escape.

One night, a mouse passed by his cage. "Hello," called Jimbo mournfully, for by now he was feeling very lonely, and no-one had cleaned his cage out for days.

"Hello!" said the mouse. "You don't look very happy. What's the matter?" Jimbo explained how he had been stolen and wanted to escape back to his own circus. The mouse listened and then said, "I'll try to help." So saying, he scampered off and soon he was back with a bunch of keys. Jimbo was astonished. "Easy!" said the mouse. "The keeper was asleep, so I helped myself."

Jimbo took the keys in his trunk and unlocked the door to the cage. He was free! "Thank you!" he called to the mouse, who was already scurrying away.

Jimbo's first thought was to get back to his own circus as fast as possible. However, he wanted to teach those thieves a lesson. He could hear them snoring in their caravan. He tiptoed up, as quietly as an elephant can tiptoe, and slid into the horse's harness at the front. "Hey, what do you think you're doing?"

neighed one of the horses, but Jimbo was already hauling the robbers' caravan out of the gate and down the road.

So gently did he pull the caravan that the thieves never once woke up. Eventually they reached Ronaldo's Circus. Mr Ronaldo was dumbstruck to see Jimbo pulling a caravan just like a horse! Mr Ronaldo walked over to the caravan and was astonished to see the robbers still fast asleep. He raced to the telephone and called the police, and it wasn't until they heard the police siren that the robbers woke up. By then it was too late. As they emerged from the caravan scratching and shaking their heads they were arrested on the spot and taken off to jail. "There are a few questions we would like to ask Mr Zipper regarding the theft of some other circus animals, too," said one of the police officers.

Mr Ronaldo, and Jimbo's keeper Carlos, were both delighted to see Jimbo back home again. And Jimbo was just as delighted to be back home. Then Mr Ronaldo and Carlos started whispering to each other and began walking away looking secretive. "We'll be back soon, we promise," they said to Jimbo. When they returned, they were pushing Jimbo's old cage. It had been freshly painted, there was clean, sweet-smelling straw inside, but best of all there was no lock on the door! "Now you can come and go as you please," said Carlos.

And Jimbo trumpeted long and loud with his trunk held high, which Carlos knew was his way of saying, "THANK YOU!"

The Sleeping Beauty

A long time ago, in a land far away, there ruled the happiest king and queen who had ever lived. They were especially happy because after years of hoping in vain, they had finally been blessed by the birth of a beautiful baby daughter.

The king and queen were so happy that they decided to celebrate by throwing a huge banquet for their family and friends, and all the most important people in the kingdom. As they sat down to write the invitations, a worried look crossed the queen's face. "The Countess Griselda will be very angry if she doesn't get an invitation," she said to her husband.

The king's face went very pale for a moment. Then he shook his head and said, "No, she must not be invited. Griselda is wicked and mean. I do not wish her to cast her eyes on our beautiful daughter." With that they continued writing the invitations.

The day of the banquet arrived, and all the most important people took their places in the Great Hall. Before the celebrations began, a line formed to pay homage to the little Princess Angelina, who lay sleeping in her cradle next to the king and queen's thrones. Twelve people stood in line, and one by one they stepped forward to give their gift to the sleeping princess.

First up stepped the good Lady Soprano, who touched the baby's throat with her forefinger and declared that the princess would have a voice like an angel. Next came the Archduke Ernest, and with a light touch on her forehead he vowed she would grow to be very wise. Next came the Duchess Rose, who stroked the baby's face and declared she would blossom into the most beautiful flower in the kingdom.

One by one the guests came forward and bestowed the gifts of patience, kindness, faith, grace, fortune, virtue, happiness and sweetness. With just one guest left to give her gift, there was a terrible noise outside the Great Hall and the huge doors were thrown open in a rage. In stormed the Countess Griselda. The Great Hall fell silent as she slowly approached the sleeping baby. The king and queen jumped to their feet to protect their little one, but Griselda swept them both aside.

As they looked up in fear at Griselda, she turned to them and whispered in a hard, cruel voice, "I think you mislaid my invitation, but I have come to give my gift to the precious child anyway." As she bent over the child she cackled, "To this child I bestow the gift of absolute health until the day she dies." As relief showed itself on the faces of the crowd, she roared with laughter and bellowed, "Which is why it is such a pity she will not live beyond her sixteenth birthday!" The crowd was stunned

as she continued, "A spindle shall be her end. A common peasant's spindle." And she touched the tip of the middle finger on the baby's right hand. She then clapped her hands together and a great roll of thunder was heard, before a terrible wind swept through the open doors blowing out all the candles. When the doors were shut and the candles re-lit, Griselda had disappeared, leaving only her terrible spell behind her.

As the king and queen wept, they did not see the final guest who had yet to bestow her gift. The Marquess Maria bent over Angelina and whispered, "I cannot take away the evil of Griselda, but I can give you the greatest gift of all. I give you the gift of love. On that terrible day to come you shall not die a death, but sleep, little one, sleep deep and peacefully as you sleep now, until love comes to rescue you." She placed her forefinger on the baby's heart and then was gone.

The king and queen were in despair, and they demanded that every spindle in the kingdom be destroyed. But they couldn't sleep a single night without worrying, and a day didn't pass that they let the little princess out of their sight for a moment.

Angelina grew, and with every passing year she became sweeter, and with every passing day she became more beautiful.

181

The day before Angelina's sixteenth birthday arrived and as the king looked at his daughter he felt a pang of sorrow, for he knew that he could not stop her destiny.

Her birthday arrived, and for the first time ever the king and queen allowed her to roam freely around the castle. The king had ordered a huge celebration to be prepared in the Great Hall for later in the day, and Angelina had tremendous fun watching the cooks prepare delicious pies, pastries and cakes in the kitchens. She watched the servants making garlands of flowers and roamed through all the corridors to watch the preparations.

In a corridor off the Great Hall, she followed a trail of petals, winding first one way and then another, up and up into a turret in the castle that she had never visited before. When she reached the top, a door swung open and in the corner of the darkened room a little old lady sat spinning some yarn.

"Come closer, my child," she beckoned.

Angelina moved closer.

"Closer still," she urged.

When Angelina was close enough the old woman

reached out to Angelina's right hand and pulled it to the spindle needle. The princess gave a gasp of pain as it pricked her middle finger, and then she fell into the deepest, most peaceful of sleeps. And as she fell asleep, the whole castle fell asleep, too. The cooks fell asleep at the roasting spit. The horses fell asleep in the stable. The king fell asleep on his throne. Everything in the castle came to a complete and utter standstill.

The years passed by, and with every passing year the thorns that grew around the castle became thicker and higher, and the legend of the sleeping beauty spread to distant lands. As time went on, many brave princes tried to cut down the thorns, but not one succeeded and countless young men were lost forever in the forest of thorns.

Many years had passed before one brave prince awoke from a dream in which the angelic voice of a strange girl had called to him from a thorn bush. He asked his father the meaning of the dream, but the king shook his head and said it was best he didn't know.

But the following night, the young prince once again dreamed of the strange girl, and this time he saw the princess deep in sleep but calling to be freed. The prince was enchanted. She was the most beautiful girl he had ever seen, and again he asked his father who she was. Again the king refused to say anything, but when the prince's dreams continued and the prince felt he would rather die than live without the princess, the king relented, and told his son of the sleeping princess far, far away.

The prince lost no time, and set off on a voyage that lasted a year and a day. Along the way he heard tales of the princes who had tried before him and the fate they had met; some had been turned to stone, some had turned to water, and others had simply vanished without trace, but none had succeeded.

The prince finally reached his destination and stood outside the walls of the thorn forest. He knelt and said a prayer for all the lost souls who had tried before him, and then he raised his sword to strike the thorns. In that instant, a vision of the princess rose up to him, and he was so overcome with love that he dropped his sword and tried to touch the vision. As he reached out he touched the thorns, and as he touched the thorns, they turned into flowers in his hands. The further into the forest he went, the more the forest bowed down before him, until all that separated him from the princess was a carpet of roses. The prince raced past the sleeping horses, cooks and the king and ran up the stairs to where the princess lay. He bent over her sleeping form and placed a single kiss upon her rosy lips. In that instant, she opened her eyes – love had set her free.

The cooks yawned at their spit and woke up. The horses neighed their yawns and woke up. The king yawned on his throne and woke up. Everyone in the castle woke up. When the prince led the princess to her father he cried with joy, and granted him any wish that he could choose. The prince asked for the princess's hand in marriage, and they both lived happily ever after.

You're Not My Best Friend

Gabriella Goat, Chicken Charlotte, Sam the Sheepdog, Penfold Pig, Sally the Sheep and Jersey Cow all lived on Willow Farm. In the late afternoon when all the farm work had been done, they liked to meet in the paddock next to the farmyard to talk.

Gabriella was a very self-important goat, because she thought she was more useful on the farm than all the other animals. Not only did she provide milk for the farmer's wife to make cheese, but she also nibbled all the nettles and weeds and kept the farmyard neat and tidy. As far as she was concerned, that was much more important that just laying eggs or looking after sheep, or helping the farmer look for truffles, growing wool, or making milk.

Each morning, when Chicken Charlotte had finished laying eggs and all the other animals were still hard at work, she would flutter over the picket fence that kept the foxes away and strut over to visit Gabriella.

One very hot day when the sun was shining down on the garden, Gabriella decided she and Chicken Charlotte should go down to the duck pond and soak their feet in the clear, cool water. Chicken Charlotte didn't like this idea at all! "I'm afraid I might fall in and drown," said Chicken Charlotte. "I can't swim."

"You can't swim?" gasped Gabriella Goat. "How can you be any fun if you can't swim?" And with that, she turned her back on Chicken Charlotte. Gabriella thought about who else liked swimming, and then smiled triumphantly. "Sam the Sheepdog can swim," she said. "In fact sheepdogs can do lots of things chickens can't. Sam will be my very best friend."

Chicken Charlotte went back to her coop feeling very miserable!

Sam the Sheepdog had just finished chasing Sally the Sheep into the field when Gabriella Goat called out to him, "How about taking a break now and coming to the duck pond with me?"

Sam scratched behind his ear and panted hard as he thought about this. "Why not?" he said when he'd got his breath back. "It's a boiling hot day and I could do with a nice long swim to help me cool down."

187

Gabriella and Sam had tremendous fun all day splashing around in the water, and at the end of the day Gabriella said to Sam, "You're my very best friend. Let's do this again tomorrow!"

Sam agreed. He was delighted that Gabriella liked him the best of all the animals.

The next day, Gabriella went to fetch Sam so that they could play. It was another very hot day and she was especially looking forward to a nice swim. Sam was in the field chasing Sally, but when Gabriella beckoned for him to come and play, Sam shook his head. "It's too early," said Sam. "I've got to make sure Sally grazes all this field, and in any case most of the water has dried out of the pond and it's all muddy. The farmer won't like it if I get too dirty."

"What?" squealed Gabriella Goat in disbelief. "Whoever heard of a dog that didn't like mud? How can you be any fun if you don't like mud?" And with that she turned her back on Sam the Sheepdog. Gabriella thought for a while about who else might like mud, and then smiled triumphantly. "Penfold Pig likes getting muddy," she said. "In fact, pigs like to do lots of things that dogs don't. Penfold Pig will be my very best friend."

Sam was too upset even to chase Sally around the field now, and he lay down with his tail between his legs feeling very miserable.

Penfold Pig was snuffling around in the hot yard when Gabriella Goat found him. "Don't bake here," said Gabriella. "Come and roll in the mud with me."

Penfold Pig was delighted at this prospect, and off they both trotted towards the muddy pool. They had such fun that Penfold wanted to do this again the following day, but Gabriella said that she'd had enough of basking now, and tomorrow she wanted to lie in the field and chew juicy grass. Penfold Pig was distraught. He didn't like chewing grass – he'd much rather eat pig-swill. Sadly, he told Gabriella Goat that he'd not be able to join her.

"Pah! Pathetic," she moaned. "You'll never make a good best friend if you can't eat grass." And with that she turned her back on Penfold Pig. She thought for a while about who else liked eating grass, and then smiled triumphantly. "Jersey Cow likes eating grass," thought Gabriella Goat. "In fact cows like eating grass all day long. Jersey Cow will be my very best friend."

Penfold Pig wallowed in the mud on his own and felt extremely miserable.

The following morning, Gabriella went to find Jersey Cow, who was just about to be milked by the farmer's wife. She told Jersey Cow her plans for the day. Jersey Cow said that she would be honoured to have Gabriella to talk to as they chomped and lazed the day away. "I'll be with you in just a tick," said Jersey Cow. "I need to be milked first."

Gabriella Goat stared at Jersey Cow, and then turned and walked away without saying anything at all! "What's wrong with all these silly animals?" she asked herself. "Why do they always have to do something else first, or can't even do something at all?" And with that she decided to go alone to the juicy green field.

When Gabriella got to the field, she spied Sally the Sheep grazing away. "At last," she thought, "there's a creature that wants to do the same as me."

Sally the Sheep was very pleased to be chosen as Gabriella's friend, and they spent the next hour talking and munching away in the heat of the sun. Before very long, Jersey Cow came to join them. But Gabriella wouldn't talk to Jersey Cow, no matter how nice Jersey Cow tried to be.

"Friendship is all about giving and taking," remarked Gabriella to Sally the Sheep (so that Jersey Cow could overhear), "and being a very best friend means giving a lot. Jersey Cow can't even give up being milked for one morning. She's no best friend of mine."

Instead of looking miserable, Jersey Cow looked angry, and when Jersey Cow moved off to chew some grass a little further away, Sally the Sheep followed her. Gabriella Goat snorted in disgust, and then bent her head to chew some more. "Who needs friends anyway?" she thought. "They're no good to anyone."

But Gabriella Goat started to feel bored. She wanted to play a game. She wanted to play chase! Chicken Charlotte was the best friend to play chase with, so she decided it was high time to make friends with her again. As it was getting quite late in the day, all the animals were together in the paddock. Gabriella Goat could see Chicken Charlotte, and so she skipped up to her to suggest a game. When she got close, however, Chicken Charlotte turned her back! Gabriella was taken aback, and so she turned to Sam the Sheepdog. Sam also turned his back. As she looked at each animal in turn, they all turned their backs.

Just then she heard Jersey Cow remark to Sally the Sheep, "You know, friendship is all about giving and taking. If a friend of mine wouldn't give as well as take, she'd be no friend of mine."

Gabriella was very upset. She skulked off to the farmyard and was utterly miserable. The more she thought, the more miserable she became. The more miserable she became, the more she realised what a terrible friend she had been. The next day she stayed in the farmyard because she was too ashamed to face her friends.

Presently, Chicken Charlotte came by and saw how miserable Gabriella Goat looked. She was soon joined by Sam the Sheepdog, Penfold Pig, Jersey Cow and Sally the Sheep. When Gabriella looked up and saw all her former friends, she sobbed, "I'm so sorry, won't you all forgive me?"

Chicken Charlotte flew to her side and gave her a big hug, and all the other animals joined in. Nobody had liked seeing her so down, and they wanted to be friends again. "I've been so silly," said Gabriella, " but now I realise you are ALL my very best friends."